THE MAGIC LINE

Further Mysteries by Elizabeth Gunn

THE MAGIC LINE

Elizabeth Gunn

This first world edition published 2012
in Great Britain and in the USA by
SEVERN HOUSE PUBLISHERS LTD of
9–15 High Street, Sutton, Surrey, England, SM1 1DF.
Trade paperback edition first published
in Great Britain and the USA 2012 by
SEVERN HOUSE PUBLISHERS LTD.

British Library Cataloguing in Publication Data

Gunn, Elizabeth, 1927-
   The magic line. – (The Sarah Burke series)
   1. Burke, Sarah (Fictitious character)–Fiction. 2. Women
   detectives–Arizona–Tucson–Fiction. 3. Thieves–
   Fiction. 4. Serial murder investigation–Fiction.
   5. Detective and mystery stories.
   I. Title II. Series
   813.6-dc22

3 1984 00302 5978

ISBN-13: 978-0-7278-8116-8 (cased)
ISBN-13: 978-1-84751-407-3 (trade paper)

Severn House Publishers support The Forest Stewardship Council [FSC],
the leading international forest certification organisation. All our titles that
are printed on Greenpeace-approved FSC-certified paper carry the FSC logo.

Typeset by Palimpsest Book Production Ltd.,
Falkirk, Stirlingshire, Scotland.
Printed and bound in Great Britain by
MPG Books Ltd., Bodmin, Cornwall.

ACKNOWLEDGMENTS

This book could never have been written without the help of Sergeant Kerry Fuller, 'first shirt' at the Westside station of the Tucson Police Department, and these members of her loyal crew: Sergeant Bob Callan, Officer Mark 'Sponge' Zbojniewicz, and Officer Russ Pope, all of whom gave me great ride-alongs and advice about procedures, firearms and scene-setting. I constantly marvel at the compassion of Tucson patrol officers for the less fortunate, and for ink-stained scribblers trying to get it right.

Because I am not a shooter, and this story includes a lot about guns, I am deeply indebted to Bongi Bishop, Forensic Firearms and Toolmark Examiner, Tucson Police Department Crime Laboratory, and to Chuck and the rest of the remarkably knowledgeable staff at Murphy's Gun Shop on Country Club Road.

For adventurous jaunts in search of just-right scenes for this book, I want to thank my patient husband, Phil Gunn, who greatly augments the pleasure of exploring Tucson's diversity.

ONE

'Yeah, but it'd be a lot safer after dark,' Zeb said.

'Ah, there goes Mr Yeah-but again.' Robin kept his eyes on the house on Spring Brook Drive. 'Put a sock in it, will you? We settled this.'

'But it's broad daylight, anybody can see—'

'What anybody? It's four o'clock, everybody on this block's at work.'

'That woman on the corner with the babies—'

'She's back in the kitchen fixing supper. We spent two weeks casing this fucker, now you can't remember anything we learned?' They argued in stifled bursts, keeping their voices low, barely audible above the A/C. Zeb was worried about keeping that running, too – conspicuous on the quiet street, he thought – but in Tucson in late May, with no shade, they'd die without air. And they had to sit here in the sun to wait – it was the best spot: close enough to watch the house, far enough not to be noticed.

'Yeah, but all along you said we'd pick the safest time—'

'Which will be fifteen seconds after these clowns are all the way into their garage, with the door rolling down. Just back from deliveries, before they get the money put away.' Robin whipped around on the seat and froze his partner in a pale, bright stare. 'You saying you want to back out now, Zeb-you-lon?'

'*No*, I don't want to back *out*, come on.' Robin always drawled his name out like that, taunting, when he wanted to put him down. It worked, too, because Zeb knew people always got major yucks out of his name. 'Zebulon Montgomery Butts, for Chrissake,' he had asked his mother on his last birthday, 'what were you thinking?' Twenty-one at last, time to get a few things straightened out.

His mother said she named him after a great man to inspire him to do great deeds, and she still had high hopes for that.

But then last month, as she piled his belongings outside her casita, she'd said, 'If you're ever going to do any of those great deeds it's sure as hell time you got started.' She put a list on top of the pile – things he had to do before she let him back in.

Number One on her Tough Love list was 'Get a job.'

Doing what? Yard care gave him back pain. Construction was in the toilet. He always got fired from resort work – high-paying customers were just too demanding to tolerate. He'd been thinking about applying for a UPS job till three months ago when that stupid DUI charge got his license suspended. Nobody seemed to understand that he was going through a rough patch.

His last girlfriend said she was 'with somebody now.' The second to last let him spend one night on her couch but said her mother was coming the next day, sorry. So Zeb begged his sister till she let him put down his sleeping bag in her utility room, as long as he used his own towel in the shower and didn't take anything out of the refrigerator.

Finally he'd looked up Robin and asked him was he up to any *mischief* these days; did he need a *boost* with anything? They used to talk like that when he teamed with Robin before – back when everything was a *caper*, a little out on the edge maybe but nothing serious. Robin had done a short stretch in juvie and hooked up with a weird kid named Hermie who could boost almost any car super fast, and was willing to teach Robin all he knew.

Zeb thought of it now as their crazy-teens period, when he was doing *capers* with Robin and Hermie. He didn't learn any new skills except how to blow a quick blast on Hermie's weird whistle. Luckily he never had to blow it while he was their lookout, but they paid him a little for standing by with it, anyway. Later, after they trusted him a little, he ferried a few of Hermie's boosted cars to chop shops. No big scores but it sure beat bagging groceries at Fry's.

Luckily, Zeb was working for his mother the night Robin and Hermie finally got caught trying to burgle a house in the Sam Hughes Neighborhood. A patrolman spotted the open window they had jimmied, looked in and shined his light on them. He kept them standing there with their hands full of high-end electronics and an antique set of dueling pistols waiting for his backup to arrive. 'Don't move,' he told them several times, but Hermie, who hated taking orders, dropped the guns at the last minute and ran out the front door into heavy traffic on Country Club Road. He got a long sentence after he got out of the hospital. Robin stayed where he was and did twenty-two months at the State Prison on Wilmot Road.

He was different when he came out – his eyes were like polished steel, and constantly scanned any room he was in. He mostly hung with guys who did martial arts and had weird facial hair – they broke into empty stores and abandoned houses and stayed till somebody chased them out, using the empty spaces to plan heists and divvy up what they stole.

Robin wasn't any fun at all to be around for quite a while after Wilmot. He never let you finish a sentence that had more than eight words in it, and some days he just seemed to be trying to start a fight for any reason. Finally Zeb decided he didn't need the grief and made a point of being where Robin wasn't.

But last month, when his mother got all crazy about jobs and put him out, Zeb thought back to the good old days and decided to look up his old pal. He tried for a light note, asking was he doing any *capers* these days? Robin gave him one of his new ice-blue looks and said capers were yesterday's news. Said he had some *jobs* from time to time but he needed somebody who was ready to *get serious*.

'Robin, come on, it's me. How long we known each other?'

'Years and years. And in all that time, you have never shown me one brilliant move.' Robin kicked his metal-clad toe against a curb while Zeb waited. 'I could try you out,' he said finally. 'Kind of on probation.'

Zeb understood probation now – the Department of Motor Vehicles had seen to that. After he'd flunked his sobriety test last winter he got lucky with a judge, who cited and released him with the stern proviso that if she saw him in her courtroom again on a similar charge he was going to spend a long time in County mending his ways. At first he'd congratulated himself on getting a judge who was such a muffin. It took him a couple of months to realize that having no driver's license didn't just keep him from driving a car, it ensured he wouldn't be considered for any job he might conceivably want.

So he put on his humble face and did every *job* Robin asked him to do. For peanuts. On time and without complaint. Nothing big; he made a few dope deliveries, lifted a set of hex wrenches from a target store.

Stealing tools off a rack didn't feel like starting to do great deeds, but he did it because he could see it was some kind of gate he had to pass through to please Robin. Hard to see what Robin wanted them for – they were still in the bubble wrap on the floor of the empty warehouse where they'd met this month. But Robin seemed pleased when he came back with them and made a weird joke about hexes. He kind of warmed up to Zeb after that, and asked if Zeb was ready for something a little bigger. When Zeb said sure, Robin said he needed help planning a home invasion.

Home invasion was kind of a scary leap into the unknown, but hell, if he wasn't going to flip burgers he had to get started at something else. They were in Robin's car – this week's car, he seemed to go through them like popcorn – headed for the neighborhood to take a look at the house, when Robin explained that the home he was planning to invade was a stash house. Right then, when Zeb's stomach cramped up, was when he should have bailed, he thought later. But he needed the money. And more than that, he wanted the connection to Robin and the feeling he was ready to step up his game a little, be a player. He hadn't slept through one whole night since, and the nightmares that woke him up kept coming back in the daytime, wrecking his digestion. But he was hanging in, determined to go through with this job.

So now he was sitting next to a peeling wooden fence on Chardonnay Drive with a good view of the house on Spring Brook Drive. Waiting in this beat-up carpet cleaner's van, with two guys named Earl and Homer. He'd only met his new team-mates and fellow home invaders yesterday, and the van he'd never seen before – Robin just showed up in it with no explanation. Zeb was sweating, feeling his heart beat. For the first time ever, Zeb was armed and, he hoped, dangerous.

'We ain't gonna unload any of this rug-cleaning shit, are we?' Earl asked Robin from back in the shady cargo space where he and his brother Homer crouched among the tools. 'You got some fuckin' heavy shit back here.'

'No,' Robin said. 'I told you. Just start the cordless vacuum for the noise, and walk up to the front door with the clipboard. Keep those pens in your pocket, like you're all ready to write up the job. Ring the bell and look polite while Homer steps out from behind you with the elephant gun and blows 'em away.' He took his eyes off the door long enough to turn and smile at Earl. 'You can look polite for just a minute, can't you?'

Homer goosed Earl. 'Yeah, Earl, you be lookin' p'lite while I shoot their fuckin' heads off, huh?' He had a weird laugh, *hyaw-hyaw-hyaw,* and one of his eyes wandered.

Zeb didn't know their last name. He'd asked Robin, 'Where'd you find Darrell-and-Darrell?'

Robin just chuckled briefly, that dry little half laugh he'd developed lately, and said, 'Don't worry about them, they'll be fine.'

Earl couldn't seem to say one whole sentence without obscenities but usually made a brutal kind of sense. Homer really did seem to be a few cards short of a deck. He was good with his weapons, Zeb would give him that. But it rubbed his nerves raw to share this cramped space with a guy who kept flipping a butterfly knife over and over, in and out of attack mode, catching the handle one-handed every time. Balisong, they called that weapon. Robin carried one too, sometimes, in a holder Velcroed to his leg. Not today, though – he was travelling light today. Stripped down for action, he told Zeb with a wink.

Finally Robin said, 'Homer, you don't quit playing with that knife I'm going to stick it up your ass,' and Homer tucked it into an ankle holster. He showed Zeb another knife he kept in a zippered pocket on the leg of his cargo pants. Then he started moving his big handgun from place to place under his shirt, making a point of telling Zeb it was a .44 Magnum Smith & Wesson revolver. He watched Zeb's face when he said it, wanting to be sure Zeb understood what a kick-ass weapon that was. Zeb didn't know much about guns but he was trying to firm up his place on the team so he looked at it respectfully and said, 'Hey, big time.'

Homer couldn't seem to decide between a shoulder holster and his belt. Then he tried out several cleaning buckets till he found one big enough to conceal the gun. He tied a couple of towels around the handle for cover so he could carry the gun inside the bucket, ready to fire. When he had it arranged to suit himself he poked Earl, chuckling, and said, 'Looky here, what'cha think?'

'Looks OK.' Earl had a pistol of some kind, under his shirt in a shoulder holster, that he seemed at ease with and never took out. As soon as he saw how much of his chest the clipboard would cover, he unbuttoned the top two buttons on his shirt. After that he sat still, looking fierce but relaxed, like a panther after lunch.

Zeb was nervous about his own weapon. Robin had given it to him last week, along with the shirt he was to wear on this job. That was a surprise too, a hiking shirt from Summit Hut with clever, hidden pockets fastened with Velcro. One of the pockets had another, zippered pocket inside. 'You get to carry the money,' Robin said, with more winking; he was making an effort to keep Zeb on his team today. Zeb got a tremor in his chest, thinking about stuffing those pockets with money. How heavy would that shirt get? He could almost feel it on his shoulders – the pull of money.

Robin said the gun was a Lorcin semi-auto, whatever the hell that meant. It fit easily in his hand and was not complicated to fire. It seemed a little small for the task at hand which, he had almost admitted to himself, might include shooting somebody who was trying to shoot him first. He had practiced at a firing range with Robin beside him, talking him through it like a drill master.

'Don't look at the gun, look at the target. Support it with both hands, so you hold it steady, see? Take a deep breath, let it out slowly . . . slow-leee . . . now squeeze. Good, you actually grazed the edge of the target that time. Can't you stop shaking?'

Later, in front of his sister's mirror while she was at work, he had watched himself pulling the handgun out of his belt and aiming. He told himself over and over, *Just pull it out, aim it and shoot.* He tried to stifle the voice in his head that kept saying, *Yeah, but the mirror's not shooting back.*

'Heads up,' Robin said now. 'Here they come.' Zeb felt hot blood rush into his head and neck; now felt way too soon. He could see two men in the front seat of the approaching Chevy Malibu, the bald one driving and the dark-haired one with the brush cut, in the passenger seat where he always sat, scanning the street with laser eyes. Zeb held his breath and craned forward, trying to see. Was there a third man in the back?

It was the question they'd never settled: were there two men in the house, or three? During two weeks of watching, they had only ever identified two men going in and out of the house. But whenever they watched the runs in the SUV, they thought they saw a third man sitting very straight in the middle of the back seat. Hard to be sure with those darkened windows, but it sure looked like there was a third guy in there again today.

Uncertainty about the third man was the reason, Robin said, why he'd added Earl and Homer.

'You think we need more firepower, huh?' Zeb said, after he met them.

'Well, yes,' Robin said. 'I probably wouldn't be counting on them for more brainpower, hmm?' Zeb snickered, Robin winked and chuckled, and for a few seconds they were buddies like old times. But then Zeb went ahead and asked what was their split going to be? Because he had already put in two weeks on this job with no cash flow, and now these two mean, pushy thugs were acting like they owned the thing.

'No split. Three hundred apiece for an hour's work, that's all they get.'

'Oh. Well, then. OK.'

'Of course OK. I know how to set up jobs, Zebby. So why don't you just chill and let me handle things?' Which Zeb did, of course, because without Robin there was no job. But something about the way these crazy, dangerous brothers cleared out space for themselves made Zeb suspect they'd been in on the deal from the beginning.

Robin didn't put the van in gear until the Malibu was in the driveway, the garage door beginning to rise. Watching that door go up, Robin had said, the stash house guys would be thinking about getting inside and wouldn't even notice the utility van rolling toward them in the street. A cargo van with a sign on the side that said 'Bestway Carpet Cleaning' was as good as invisible.

The Bestway van was still two doors away when the garage door began to roll back down. It was closed by the time Robin pulled up at the foot of the driveway and parked. Earl hit the switch on the big vacuum and they swung the rear doors open so the sound of air roaring through the hose filled the street. They got out, Earl with his clipboard up in front of his chest and Homer with the towels hiding the revolver in the bucket, and walked sedately up the driveway.

Robin and Zeb had already trotted up the driveway and along the side of the house to the backyard. That was the plan, for the two of them to get around in the back while the men inside were still in the garage. Zeb carried the glass cutter in his fist, so it didn't show. Robin had the suction cup under his big shirt, on a cord around his neck.

'That lady on the corner's coming outside,' Zeb said.

'She's just getting the mail,' Robin said. 'She'll go right back in to the babies, forget about her.'

Earl and Homer were almost at the front door. Earl had his pens on a pocket protector, his brutal face screwed into a weird little smile above the clipboard. The heavy-duty metal door, double locked, the only really secure door on this working-class street of cheap, ageing bungalows, had pulled Robin to this stash house like a magnet.

Back of the house, on the cement slab that passed for a patio, they saw the blinds were closed like always inside the sliding glass door. That's what Robin liked so much about this job: the way the men running this stash house kept everything in the back closed up tight. The door and the double window overlooking the yard were always shut and locked, blinds down, drapes closed.

For two weeks Zeb had biked and driven around this house and hidden in the empty house with the 'For Sale' sign three doors away. He had never seen anyone look out the back window or walk out the sliding door and sit on the cement by the dying cactus.

'Dumb shits think it keeps them safe to keep the blinds closed,' Robin had said, grinning at the weed-choked backyard the last time they watched it. 'Just makes our job easier.'

Watching the window now, smiling the odd, humorless smile Zeb had noticed on him lately, Robin pulled on surgical gloves. *Why don't I have some of those?* Zeb wanted to ask but didn't dare start an argument now.

Robin pulled the suction cup out from under his shirt – the roomy blue denim shirt that he had bought in a thrift shop just for this job. Gathered below a broad yoke, it looked old-fashioned like the Dutch Boy on paint cans, but had a modern left sleeve with a zippered small iPod pocket where Robin kept his radio. 'Radio's better than an iPod,' he said. 'I can get anything I want on it and nobody can trace it.' Not being traceable, Zeb noticed, had become very important to Robin.

He set the suction cup in place on the window, six inches from the latch. It was actually called a dent puller, but glass installers used them, too. He'd ordered it from Amazon – $2.39 plus shipping, he'd told Zeb, chuckling, and there wouldn't be a local record of the purchase. Robin thought of everything these days; there was a new little line between his eyebrows and when he wasn't smiling that too-wide smile under the bright eyes, one side of his mouth had begun to turn down in something like a snarl.

Zeb cut a big circle around the suction cup with the glass cutter. One little squeak was all the noise it made. He could hear people moving around inside, and some quiet talk he couldn't understand. A drawer opened somewhere near the window. Some rustling, then the drawer slid closed and the drawer-pull clicked against the plate. Zeb felt as if his ears were growing.

Robin pulled on the suction cup. Nothing moved. He turned his bright eyes on Zeb and mouthed, *Tap it*. Zeb laid three fingers of his left hand on the glass, tapped them once lightly with the handle of the cutter, and felt the glass move. Robin pulled out the circle, set it quietly on the cement, and replaced the suction cup very carefully in the center of the circle on the inside pane. Zeb began cutting around the cup, close this time, working carefully so he didn't cut himself on the outer glass.

The doorbell rang: chimes, a little tune.

A voice inside, quite near, said something like 'Who the fuck's that?' softly, like he was deciding whether to answer it or not.

Footsteps – two sets or three? Zeb couldn't decide. He finished the second cut and Robin hit the puller gently with the heel of his hand. When the glass gave he pulled the circle out, set it down, stuck his hand inside and slowly, gritting his teeth in concentration while he listened, raised the latch. It rolled up without a sound. Zeb, who hadn't known he was holding his breath, exhaled.

A different voice, from further forward in the house said, 'Carpet cleaners. Must have the wrong house.'

The first voice, moving away, said, 'Or maybe not. Wait'll I get the—' Zeb couldn't understand the next word. Slowly, ready to stop if he made a noise, Robin slid the window sideways. Dusty venetian blinds hung just to the waist-high sill. Robin moved one slat aside an inch and they saw a stained cotton lining inside a flowered drape. Robin nodded, looking pleased, and turned his back to the opening. He set both hands behind him on the sill, hoisted his butt onto it, mouthed, *Let's go*, turned sideways and swung one leg over.

Inside there was some quiet scurrying, a hinge squealed on what sounded like a cupboard, and the doorbell rang again. There was a whoosh of air as the front door opened and the blind and drape bellied out the open window. Robin was briefly wrapped inside plastic slats and the clinging drape. He pushed it all away and swung his other leg inside. Homer's big gun roared at the front door; Earl's barked right behind it. Another gun answered from inside and then a chattering weapon cut loose and drowned out everything else. Somebody screamed in the front yard. Robin dropped inside, ducked under the blind and disappeared.

Zeb turned his back to the window sill, ready to push himself up and follow Robin into the house. But then there was another great burst of gunfire, and a bullet blew through the left side of the back window, close to the jamb, carrying fragments of flowered drape and plastic blind along with many shards of glass. He felt the wind as it passed his head, and a sliver of glass lodged in his cheek.

The screaming out front stopped abruptly. There was one more shot inside the house, then silence. And then Zeb heard, from somewhere amazingly close and coming on fast, a siren. It felt like a knife slicing into his brain – the cops were already here!

He ran like a rabbit. Dropping his glass-cutting tool on the cement, he abandoned Robin, great deeds and easy money – the money he had imagined so clearly, he would have sworn he could feel it weighing down his special pockets.

There was a break in the wooden fence, down by the corner post. Not large, but he sucked up his gut, held his breath and slithered into the neighbor's yard. He ducked under sheets on a clothes line, climbed through a wire fence into another yard that was open to the street. Running east on Chardonnay Drive he reached Oak Tree Drive and ran south along it, his tattoos and body piercings flashing in the late-afternoon sun.

A second patrol car turned into the street, siren screaming. Zeb saw him slow at the sight of a running man, muttered, 'Oh, shit,' and began looking for a yard to duck into. But the car's radio clattered with urgent orders, 'ten-ninety-nine, see the officer at . . .' and the address on Spring Brook Drive. Zeb saw a flash, marveled that a patrolman would shoot through his own windshield, then realized he had not been shot and a second later knew he'd just been photographed. No sweat, he thought, a blurry photo of a running man, so what? What mattered was the black-and-white drove on.

The scare did him a favor actually, made him realize running was conspicuous. As soon as he slowed to a walk he remembered the Lorcin was still in the waistband of his pants. He stuck it in his pocket and walked briskly into the parking lot of the Walmart Store, doing his best to look unarmed and harmless. Inside the sliding front doors of the store he stood still, feeling his sweat cool.

His pockets yielded a few rumpled bills. He counted them

carefully, tucked them in a safe pocket and found the men's clothing section. He bought a T-shirt in size XL that said 'Go Wildcats' and looked like it would cover most of his tats, found a baseball cap with a Diamondbacks logo, and picked out the biggest pair of sunglasses on a rack.

After he changed in the restroom he stuffed his sweat-soaked, many-pocketed Money Bag shirt into one of the Walmart bags and dropped it in the trash can near the door. Carrying a tall iced drink from a vending machine, he went outside and found a bench under a mesquite tree.

Sipping his drink in the busy parking lot, he did what his mother had been urging him to do for some time. He thought hard about his situation.

TWO

Sarah Burke, driving home, heard the heads-up tone on her radio and felt her pulse jump. Out of long habit, Sarah's muscles grew tight, her whole body getting ready to act.

Seconds after the tone ended, the radio rattled with urgent orders to patrol cars. Something big was happening on the south end of town – 'See the woman' and reports of shooting at an address in the Midvale Park district.

Forget it, she told herself. Urgent call-outs were not her problem anymore. Being a homicide detective was no cake walk, but at least she was no longer expected to turn on her siren and race to crime scenes. And she had earned the treat she was headed for – getting home to Bentley Street in plenty of time for dinner. She'd even left a little unfinished work on her desk and cut out early, because she'd been called to a crime scene at six that morning and the department was insisting that detectives avoid overtime whenever possible.

Inside her front door she called hello and walked into her bedroom to lock her Glock and shield away. She hung up her work clothes, got into a soft old T-shirt and shorts. Stretching and yawning, she got comfortable, slowed down and began the transition to non-vigilent, slack-jawed civilian. 'Releasing my inner slob,' her buddy Kate Kerry called it. Kate was a shift commander now on the West Side, but they had gone through training together and remained close. 'Coming down from cop mode used to be a tough transition,' Kate boasted, 'but these days, let me get barefoot in something with a stretch waistband – I can turn into a couch potato in under five minutes.' Sarah wasn't quite that down with it yet, but getting close.

Hearing voices where her family was clustered, in the kitchen end of the house, Sarah walked toward them, saying, 'Something smells good and I am so ready to stick a fork in it.'

Will Dietz sat by a window in the old wooden rocker, a relic from the ranch of Sarah's childhood that was becoming his favorite chair in this house. Only his feet and hands showed; the rest of him was buried in the morning paper. She touched his shoulder as she passed him and he made a small sound, 'Mmff.' This being Monday, he'd go back to work with his night detectives' squad in a couple of hours. Monday through Thursday, they saw each other only in passing. He spent most of his afternoons puttering with shelves and closets, doorsills and moldings, getting them settled in this sixty-year-old house they'd just moved into.

'Come and taste this, will you?' Aggie said, out in the kitchen by the stove. 'Tell me if it needs more of anything besides salt.' Recovering from a stroke, Sarah's mother had resumed cooking but told them all to add their own salt.

'Ah, meat sauce, good.' Sarah leaned over the pan, sniffing the garlicky steam. 'And what's that, penne? Wonderful.' Pleasure in the food didn't quite block the little spurt of alarm she often felt these days when she stood close to Aggie. *Damn, she seems to keep shrinking.*

'Points off if you drool in the sauce,' Denny said, setting the table.

'Too late,' Sarah said. 'I worked all day on a prune Danish and a Clif bar. Your dear old auntie is a ravenous beast.' She mimed fangs and claws and Denny giggled.

'The kid is checking deportment now, do you love it?' Aggie blew on a small pasta cylinder, stuck it in her mouth and muttered, 'Not quite.' She wasn't annoyed; she and Sarah had agreed they were glad to see Denny begin to show a little sass. When they joined forces to take the child in last fall, living with her substance-abusing mother had left her skinny and silent, pulling her own hair out and scratching sores on one thumb.

Will said, from deep inside the sports section, 'You work all day on that Circle K thing?'

'Uh-huh.'

'Kinda toasty in that parking lot this afternoon?'

'Yep.' When he turned a page she got a glimpse of the pink scar that slanted across his scalp, like a second part in his mouse-colored hair.

Quiet again. What is it?

Will had talked her into moving all of them into this house, insisting he had no problem living with her fragile mother and abandoned niece. She had put aside her doubts because the arrangement solved so many time and money problems. But their unlikely household vibrated sometimes with competing needs – the wall calendar in the kitchen was covered with Aggie's doctor's appointments and Denny's school events, which had to be combined with Will's night shifts and Sarah's unpredictable schedule as a homicide detective. *Fifty ways to lose a lover*, Sarah had thought more than once.

The personal relationships seemed to be working fine, though. Aggie in recovery, Denny powering through fifth grade; both relied on Will for everything from kitchen repairs to moral support at soccer games. And he seemed to enjoy his role as fixer and factotum. But the last couple of weeks he'd turned even quieter than usual. They were still fine in bed, the rare times they got there together. But plainly, Will was thinking about something. Sarah was waiting for one of their infrequent private times to find out what it was.

'OK, soup's on,' Aggie said. They each took a plate as she dished up, and moved to the round table Aggie had brought with her from her house in Marana. It was becoming a focus of their family life, almost constantly in use for meals, homework, card games and conversation. Denny had dictated its placement in the bay window near the kitchen. Sarah hung bird feeders in the trees outside, and the centerpiece was usually a pile of bird books. Sitting there, Aggie said, felt like a picnic without ants.

Left to themselves, Will and Sarah might have talked about work, but Aggie claimed the details of law enforcement ruined her appetite and Sarah thought Denny was beginning to enjoy them a little too much. So she asked Will about his efforts to get their air conditioning up to speed, and he explained why he thought the main duct had a block in it somewhere.

'I know all about blocks,' Denny said quickly. 'I've got a kid in my class who's got a logic block in his brain.' She liked Will's cop stories but had told Sarah she thought she could live without another word about house maintenance ever.

'How do you know?' Aggie finally asked, since both Will and Sarah had ignored her interruption and were still discussing ducts. 'What does it make him do?'

'He says dumb stuff like "I believe Italy's in South America." And when we tell him that's wrong and show him a map,' Denny rolled her eyes to the ceiling, 'he says that's not the Italy he's talking about.'

'You probably need to soak his head,' Aggie said.

Denny said, 'I think that's called waterboarding now, Gram.'

The phone rang. Will answered, said, 'Yes,' and passed it to Sarah.

'Burke,' Sarah said.

Delaney said, 'Sorry to do this to you.'

Will made a pot of strong coffee. Sarah drank a cup while she dressed and took the rest along in a thermos. Aggie nuked a soft taco, rolled the last of Sarah's dinner in it and handed it to her, wrapped in foil, as she left the house. She ate it, making small sounds of pleasure during the twenty minutes it took her to reach the already swarming crime scene in the Midvale Park neighborhood.

Recession had hit this part of town hard. Ten years ago it had been a thriving blue-collar area of modest single-family houses, its parks and playgrounds noisy with healthy kids and pregnant mothers. Now roofs were breaking down, gates sagged on peeling fences and cars on blocks littered some of the yards. And the drug trade was moving in.

'You're the closest of my crew I can find,' Delaney had said, 'so will you go as soon as you can? The lab crew should be there already, and Ollie'll be right behind you. He's up on the north side. I'm down in Green Valley at a swim meet with Dylan; I'll come as soon as I can find a ride home for him. Everybody else is out someplace. I'll keep after them – we're going to need everybody for this one.'

They said nothing about being tired. What was the use? It just dragged you down, made it worse.

The street was blocked at both ends. An officer stood by the barriers on Chardonnay, directing traffic and giving cryptic answers to long questions. Sarah showed him her badge. He held up the crime scene tape so she could drive underneath it and pointed to the little parking that was left.

There was the usual bustle of dark blue uniforms, vehicles coming and going. An information officer made the rounds inside the tape, carrying a recorder and notebook, getting enough preliminary information to feed the evening news shows. Sarah saw Gloria Jackson's bright copper curls bobbing and swooping above a body in the front yard, a camera at her eye. So the lab crew had arrived.

The officer on the tape copied her badge number and timed her in. He was new this year; she'd only met him once. But rookie cops liked to be remembered. Sarah squinted a minute and pulled up his name, Bobby Clark.

'How many victims, Bobby, do you know?'

'Two out here in the yard,' he said. 'I never got inside before they put me to work on the tape here, but I heard three in the house.'

'Who's the field sergeant?'

'Oh, um, it's that old guy . . . Zimmerman. Over there near the door.'

'I see him. Thanks.' She located a chevron on a blue sleeve and walked toward Phil Zimmerman, a little jolted to hear him described as 'that old guy.' *I guess he is getting kind of lean and grizzled.* But for her the sergeant still had the powerful aura she'd admired when she was a rookie – strong, capable, always on an even keel.

Behind him, on the blood-drenched front doorsill, a heavy handgun with a brass slide lay beside the dead body of a bald white male. Zimmerman squinted at his phone as he punched in a message.

Sarah said, 'Hey, Zimmy.'

He held up one finger and said, 'Lemme finish this so I don't have to . . .' and went on texting. She waited till he quit punching buttons, closed his phone and said, 'Sarah B, how you been?' He still used her nickname from ten years ago, when there had been three Sarahs on patrol in Tucson.

'Medium well.' She was glad to see him on this wild scene – though come to think of it he had transferred to the East

Side some time last year. 'How come you're pulling field sergeant duty way down here?'

'You heard about the Great Recession? We're only down about twenty guys on this shift. The duty sarge said she didn't have anybody else to send. She said, "Run over there and supervise that crew for a couple hours, till Delaney gets there."'

'Which is going to be a while yet, I'm afraid. He was still in Green Valley when he called me. So what do we have here?'

'Well, we're calling it a home invasion but as you see . . .' He gestured toward the house front full of bullet holes, the door gaping open on carnage, 'this was no ordinary home.'

'Stash house, huh?'

'One bedroom stacked high with weed. Little over a liter of coke and some paraphernalia in the kitchen. Two victims out here in the yard and three in the house. Enough weapons and ammo to start a war and it looks like it did.'

'Who got the first call?'

'Barry White. He's down there by the body near the sidewalk – you want to talk to him first?'

'Might as well. I don't know him – is he new?'

'Yeah. Recruit from Sierra Vista, wanted to try a bigger town. Here, I'll introduce you.' He walked with her down the yard and told the square-cut young patrolman in a too-tight uniform, 'Sarah's the first detective here. You were the first responder, right?'

'That's right. That house on the corner called it in. Number one female in there with two babies, hiding under the bed with them when I got there, scared to come out. Name's Josephina Quintana.'

'Did she see the shooting?'

'Um . . . hard to tell. Even after she came out from under the bed she didn't want to talk, just kept saying, "You fix, OK?" Probably got no papers.'

'So . . . you're getting a quick indoctrination in the big city.'

'Tell me about it. Two blocks away when I got the call, I got here in just over a minute. Yard was still full of smoke! The whole place smelled like a firing line. I called for backup right away.'

'Who was your first backup?'

'That's him over there, Barney Gross. You'll want to talk to him, too. He says he saw a guy running along Oak Tree Drive as he approached. He was told he was needed over here urgently, so he chose not to pursue.'

'How urgent was it?'

'Turned out I didn't really need him at all. Everybody that's lying here now was dead when I arrived. We went around this yard very cautiously and then cleared the house, but not one of them ever moved; nobody had a pulse. From the first shot to the last heartbeat, this entire incident must have gone down in less than ten minutes.'

'Wow.' Her eyes met Phil Zimmerman's for a bleak moment. 'Everybody's getting better at this, huh?'

'Uh-huh. Practice makes perfect.'

'And from what I hear we'll all be getting more practice soon.' There had been fifteen homicides in Tucson in the past thirty days, and the department had received notice that the city council would soon be forced to make further cuts in the budget.

She thanked Barry White and walked back to the house with Zimmerman, making notes as she walked. He knew what she needed for a warrant and fed her information in a steady stream, without waiting for questions.

'The two out here . . .' Zimmerman pointed toward the bodies, which were still being photographed. 'The nearest one, looks like he got blown away from the step as soon as the door opened, shot several times in the face and chest and landed on his back with his hands up. The one at the bottom of the yard must have been a real fighter; looks to me like he stood here shooting in the door till he was out of ammo. Then he put on a burst of speed and made it almost out of the yard. He's got maybe a dozen bullets in him, Sarah; it's hard to tell with all the blood but he's all shot to pieces.'

'You got any idea who killed the last man standing?'

'Good question. Better hope Forensics tell you.'

Sarah looked around. 'The ME's not here yet?'

'Nope. I called but you know . . . they're always busy. Fire & Rescue truck roared up a few minutes ago, ready to lend a hand. I sent them packing before they could mess up your crime scene.'

'Thank you very much. You ready to show me what you know?'

'Well, I am, but the lab crew's still taking pictures everywhere – let's wait a few minutes.'

'OK. I wonder if I can still catch a judge working? Maybe save a wait for a warrant.' She made some quick notes while she waited for Judge Berkowitz to come to the phone. When he answered she dictated a warrant for the house, front and back yards, attached garage and all its contents. 'And let's include the carpet cleaning van that's parked at the bottom of the driveway. I don't know what it's doing there but just in case.'

'Absolutely, let no floor scrubber go unscrutinized,' the judge said. 'It seems to me your life gets more interesting all the time, Sarah. Isn't this your second search warrant today?'

'Yes, Judge. We're all staying limber this month.'

'Shoot as many suspects as you can, will you? My calendar's crazy already.'

By the time she had his initials on the warrant form, Zimmy was back, saying, 'OK, I guess we can start in the back.'

'What, more bodies in the back of the house?'

'No. Walk right behind me, close to the wall, and I'll show you.'

She followed his heels over sparse gravel, around the corner to a small, barren backyard where she found herself staring down at glass circles and cutting tools. 'What's this? Somebody was breaking in while the house was being attacked from the front?'

'Two-pronged attack, as they say.' Zimmy made a small, ironic shrug. 'Kind of unusual, but not a bad plan, at that.'

'Well, but . . . how many did you say were inside?'

'Three. All together, right inside the door.'

'Like they were all together to start with?'

'Who knows? This open window says one of them might have come in from back here.'

Sarah stared at the neat circles on the ground. 'So you figure one man was cutting holes in the glass back here, while the other two tried to fight their way in the front?' It sounded crazy when she said it out loud. Who cuts glass during a shooting war?

'Well, there was also the man running away.'

'But you don't know for sure he was running from here.'

'Damn funny coincidence otherwise.'

'True. Has the lab crew been inside?'

He nodded. 'That red-haired girl with the camera. I don't know about prints.'

'That'll take all night, I'm not going to wait for that. Is this back door unlocked?'

'Yeah, we opened it when we saw the window.'

'It was locked until then?'

'That's right.'

'Let's go back out front and ask Gloria if we can go in.'

By the front door again she said, 'Gloria?' to the elegant backside of the six-foot self-designated 'Glamma Tech,' stretching her skintight uniform pants to get a better photo of a yellow plastic bucket and green towel on the ground a few feet from the door.

Gloria said, 'Say wha'?' without looking up. Pulled both ways between hardscrabble roots in South LA and the chemistry degree at UA she was working toward, she still talked a little ghetto sometimes. 'Got to maintain my edge,' she had told Sarah. 'Don't want to go all country like these Tucson cowboys.'

Sarah asked her now, 'You finished photographing inside?'

'Well, I did the bodies. Zimmy said they's all dead so I thought . . . whaddya *want*?' she said, standing up hipshot, frowning. It was amazing, Sarah thought, how much funky chic Gloria managed to impart to a tech's uniform.

'Just information. Don't let me distract you just when you've got that bucket right where you want it.'

'This bucket got shot in the bottom, let's give it some respect. You can go inside,' she said, turning back to her work, 'just don't breathe. We got a lot of dusting to do in there.'

'That one's got a mouth on her, hasn't she?' Zimmerman said. They followed their own track around the house again. At the back door, they put on plastic booties and gloves. Inside, she followed Zimmie's lead. 'If you can stay out of this blood spatter here . . . now step over the feet of the guy in the doorway, stand by the wall there . . .' They stretched, pivoted, hopped to reach the dry spots where they could see without doing any harm.

As Zimmerman had said, the three inside the house were close together. The big man sprawled over the doorsill must have taken a hit in the midsection, doubled up and fallen forward. The rest of his wounds appeared to be stitched across his shoulders and back. His shaved head and what she could see of his face appeared undamaged. He wore several small gold rings in each ear and had the massive shoulder and arm muscles of a bodybuilder or wrestler. His arms, from wrist to shoulder, were covered with tattoos: elaborate, skilfully drawn and tastefully tinted – a small fortune in skin art.

The second man lay on his left side, three feet behind the first. An assault rifle was near his outstretched hands, as if he'd dropped it when he fell. He must have been firing out the doorway after the first man fell.

'Had the weapon on full auto, looks like,' Zimmy said, 'spraying bullets in an arc across the two men in the yard. Bullets hit the doorjamb on both sides at the end of each swing, see?'

'Yeah. Hard to see how anybody got a shot in through a wall of fire like that, but one of them must have, huh?'

He'd worn his thick dark hair in a short brush cut and had a soul patch and a carefully trimmed line of beard that traced the outline of his jaw. His jeans were Tommy Hilfiger and his Dan Post boots had a spit shine – he had cared a lot about his appearance, which was amazingly unmarked except by two congealed lines of blood that ran down his face from a crease in his scalp. More blood had erupted out of his mouth, soaking the man beneath him.

'That cut on his scalp isn't very deep,' Zimmy said. 'That can't be what killed him, but I don't see anything else, do you?'

'No.'

The third man had ended up almost entirely under the second. As if they went down together at almost the same instant. *Maybe the same bullet?* But then why would they end up head to toe like that? The third man must have been hit first, been already falling a second or two before his partner got hit. She could see his nose and one hand, just poking out on the other side of the top man's thighs.

'How come the bottom one's wearing latex gloves? The other two aren't.'

Zimmerman said, 'Maybe he's an invader?'

'Broke in just in time to get shot by his team-mates out front?' Sarah bent lower for a closer view. 'Some game plan, huh?'

Zimmy treated her to the wry smile of the seen-it-all-twice patrolman. 'I don't think there's an entrance exam for home invaders.'

The bottom victim's feet were extended toward the back wall. The head of the man on top rested on the lower one's knees. Blood had pooled under the two of them, soaking their clothing, smearing their weapons and the two casings she saw glinting in the gore.

If they fell at the same time why didn't they bump? But if they smacked into each other you'd think they'd fall away from each other . . .

'The ME's here,' Gloria said, poking her head in. 'He says so many bodies and it's gonna get dark pretty soon, he's going to take them all down to the morgue right away and examine them there. Anything in particular you want to know about the bodies, besides everything?'

'The position of that body underneath . . . it's hard to under-stand; I can't see how he fell the way he did,' Sarah said. 'Did you get plenty of pictures in here?'

'Hundreds,' Gloria said.

'Straight down?' Sarah asked her. 'Did you take any from directly overhead?'

'Several. Sarah, I *got it*,' Gloria said, and then, with shock on her face, 'Whoa, what's happening?'

A hand had moved. Was moving. The gloved hand of the body underneath jerked forward . . .

'Rigor mortis starting,' Zimmerman said. 'Sure is early, though.'

Next to the hand, the head of the man underneath pushed

forward a couple of inches. Then the weight of the body above it shifted, rolled off a little. The head of the lower man turned up toward Sarah, who leaned above it. The eyes opened a slit in the blood-smeared face – glinted, where they caught the light.

A tongue snaked out to lick dry lips. Then a whisper: 'Who are you?'

THREE

When a patrol car circled the Walmart parking lot, Zeb had to grip the bench and talk to himself to keep from running. If that patrolman who took his picture had transmitted it to all the cars . . . Zeb hung out with a guy who got arrested a couple of months ago for possession of a controlled substance plus paraphernalia. After his parents won his release all he seemed to want to talk about was the awesome camera equipment in patrol cars now. Took front- and rear-view stills and video, he said. Zeb had seen the flash, so he knew he'd been photographed.

Now, every black-and-white he saw, Zeb felt like the driver was noting his resemblance to that picture.

It was time to move, anyway. That rosy glow from the setting sun wouldn't last much longer. All his instincts were telling him to get inside before dark – he was too tired to deal with the predatory creatures of the night. And he felt much too furtive to enjoy the glorious desert sunset painting the western sky.

He walked to the Sun-Tran bus stop in front of the Blockbuster store, got on the next bus marked 'Downtown,' and paid with a handful of coins, almost his last. He rode it to the stop on Valencia that was nearest to his sister's address and walked half a block to her apartment. She lived in a featureless stucco block of cheap rentals with high turnover, where the occupants avoided eye contact and seldom spoke. Zeb had always thought she had picked a soul-sucking place to live, but tonight he was grateful for the cold indifference of the people around him.

There were no lights on in his sister's apartment. He paused just inside the door, listened, heard only silence. The door to Janet's bedroom stood open so she wasn't in there. OK, she wasn't home from work yet but she might be any minute. He crept into her kitchen, tore one paper towel off a roll under a cupboard and quickly loaded into it whatever he could see that she might not miss – a few crackers, one carrot, a handful of raisins and some peanuts out of a can. Careful not to spill anything, he scuttled into the laundry room where he took off his shoes and dark glasses, sat down on his folded sleeping bag and ate his meager picnic. As soon as he finished, he slid into the bag and covered his head with the flap.

In the dark bag, feeling a lot like a rodent in a nest, he began to think scurrying, mouse-like thoughts. *Is Robin dead or what?* He couldn't think of a way to find out without exposing himself to risk. He didn't care if the other two men on the job were alive or dead. Except . . . *could they ID me?* They didn't know his last name. Might not even remember his first . . . *Yes, they would.* Robin had called him, tauntingly, *Zeb-you-lon.* They might not be mental giants but one of them was sure to remember that.

His name was on the arrest record for the DUI. And how many Zebulons were likely to be living in Tucson at this moment? If some detective put it together, found his picture . . . he imagined Darrell-and-Darrell, nudging and leering as they picked his picture out of a line-up, the way people did on TV. Offered any incentive, maybe a little relief at sentencing, they would jump at the chance.

He thrashed around in the bag for a few minutes, feeling as if he ought to get up, find a newspaper or turn on the TV – there must be some news by now about the shooting. But Janet might come home any minute and she'd throw a fit if she found him any place in the apartment but the laundry or bathroom. Fright had killed his hunger all day and the scanty feast he'd just eaten satisfied the little that had come back. He was comfortable for the first time in fourteen hours. It had been a long, hard day and the laundry room was dark and quiet. In a few minutes he was snoring.

FOUR

The first ten minutes after the third man opened his eyes were utterly crazy. Gloria ran and told the ME they had a live one, hold up a minute. Greenberg, cursing about gross ineptitude taking up his time, began rechecking vital signs on the other four bodies. Zimmerman placed a call to turn around the rescue squad he'd just sent away, and in less than a minute they heard its siren coming back.

Zimmerman was indignant, insisting, 'This man was dead before, I know he was dead.' He leaned above the not-quite-dead victim, asking, 'What's your name, son?' He got no answer and had to stand back, reluctantly, when the paramedic and driver came in with the wheeled cot.

'Wait a minute,' Sarah said as they got ready to buckle the restraint straps, 'I need to pat him down first.'

The paramedic, whose ID tag said his name was Blake, was scrubbed, buffed up and impatient. He said, 'Didn't he just regain consciousness?'

'Yes. But now he's not a victim, he's a suspect, and I'm not letting him out of here without patting him down.'

Sarah began groping under the big bloody shirt. 'Come on, Detective,' Blake said, 'you trying to save his life or make love to him?'

'Just wait one damn minute.' She searched on down to the ankles and stepped back. 'OK, he's yours.' While Blake and his driver maneuvered through all the obstacles in the yard to get the gurney back to the rescue truck, Zimmerman recruited an officer out of the yard crew to escort the patient-prisoner. Sarah watched them, wishing she'd taken off his boots. But the big red truck was already pulling away.

Well, we couldn't let him die here. There'd be outrage, a scandal about the crew that let a victim die while they walked around him investigating a crime. So they'd given priority to speed. Get him to the hospital, let somebody there patch up whatever was wrong with him. Decide later if he was an attacker or a defender. It was certainly the right thing to do, but every single move while she did it felt wrong.

Ollie Greenaway stepped in over the bloody doorsill, looked around bemused and said, 'Dear me, looks like we had some serious gunplay right here in the Old Pueblo.'

'Fairly serious. Four dead, so far.'

'What, have the Mexican drug wars spilled over into our peaceful little community again?'

'Kind of looks that way.' Ollie liked to ridicule the way Arizona politicians, brushing aside Tucson's long-established position in the drug market, now blamed all drug violence on the cartel wars currently raging across the border.

He was right about the hypocrisy. The drug sales were on the American side. The money came from the US, as well as most of the guns. So why call it 'the Mexican drug wars?' *Anyway, it is what it is – almost everything we say about it is a waste of breath.*

Drug dealers, gun dealers, dealers in human transport – they all knew the US–Mexican border was the honey pot, the mark-up line where the price went up for whatever you were carrying. Guns and money going south, drugs and people coming north, the border worked equally well for illegal traffickers in both directions. You could double your money carrying stuff across the border. And the border was sixty-five miles from Tucson.

Tucson cops were stuck with cleaning up the mess illegal traffic left behind. No point in crying about it. Ollie himself, when he wasn't pissed about a night call-back, had been known to point out ironically that the drug trade was job security for them, too.

A burst of loud talk erupted at the bottom of the front yard. Ollie said, 'What's Zimmy spazzing out about?'

'Oh . . . one of his death reports turned out to be somewhat exaggerated.'

Phil Zimmerman was standing out by the tape, red-faced and defensive as he turned the scene over to Sergeant Delaney, who must have found his son a ride quickly and burned a lot of rubber on I-19. Across all the hubbub in the yard she could hear Zimmy protesting, 'I've never made a bad death call before. There's something freaky about that guy, Ross. Make damn sure you keep a guard on him.'

'Like Delaney would need to be told,' Ollie muttered. His amiable freckled face scanned the room. 'Tell me about this crime scene, will you? I don't think I've ever seen such a strange arrangement of bodies.'

The two bodies in the yard were in body bags now, being loaded aboard the ME's van. But in the house, the sudden emergency of a waking dead man had taken precedence over everything else. The two remaining corpses in the house had been moved end to end next to the wall, in order to get the revived one out the door.

'This crime scene has been utterly corrupted,' Sarah said. 'You just missed a crazy mix-up.' She told him about the corpse that woke up. 'Luckily, Gloria got in here early and got a ton of pictures. So please, just wipe this picture out of your mind and wait for the one you'll get tomorrow.'

'OK, I'm standing here not remembering two bodies by a wall.' He posed with his tongue out, looking brain-dead. 'Now tell me what went on here.'

'Well, the ex-dead-guy—'

'Ex-dead-guy? Is that a new classification? It's not exactly the same as a survivor, is it?'

'Boy, is it ever not. The man on the bottom was dead, we all agreed he was dead, until suddenly he wasn't. Then we had to get him to a hospital fast! So we just completely disrupted this crime scene we'd been walking around so carefully for an hour.' She pondered the two remaining bodies in the room. 'None of these still-very-dead-guys are Mexican, by the way. All white. And they look home-grown, to me, but I don't know any of them. Do you?'

'No. But hey, you can't expect to know every drug dealer in Tucson, no matter how good your social life is.' Ollie was in a jumpy, jokey mood. He had probably had two or three beers at home to relax after their long hard day on hot asphalt, Sarah guessed. Enough to get good and sleepy. After the call to the second scene he had obviously goosed himself back up, using humor and probably an upper of some kind with a Red

Bull chaser. She was already wishing she didn't have to be around him in a couple of hours when he started to crash.

'Well, this sure is a pile of crap, isn't it?' Delaney said, walking in. 'Plenty to do here to begin with, without getting an emergency rescue crew stuck in the middle of it. The fire-house chief's already called to ask me what's going on over here – how come they got sent away and then called back. He says remember every time they take that rig out it costs a bunch of money.'

'Well, we couldn't just let the guy lie here and bleed out,' Sarah said.

'I'm not saying you did wrong. It's lucky all the systems were in place to fix the mistake.' He cleared his throat and, apparently, his brain as well, looking down at a list he had already started. 'So let's see, Sarah, you take the primary on this, please, you've already got a head start on the information. You'll have to watch a lot of autopsies, I'm afraid. I'll give Leo the scene – except, Ollie, I want you to take charge of all the guns and ammo, because you're the quickest with that.'

'And somebody better be,' Ollie said. 'I see casings every-where I look.'

'Not to mention all the bullets you're going to have to dig out of this building,' Delaney said. 'I think I'll give you Jason to help with that, or you could be here digging ammo for a week. The rest of the guys, when they get here, can start on the perimeter, canvass the neighborhood. Let's see, Zimmy said there's dope in here?'

'Spare bedroom – right back here. And the kitchen.' She showed him.

'You called the narcotics squad?'

'Not yet. I thought it could wait till we got the bodies cleared out of here. The pot's not going anyplace.'

'What about money? Must be some here.'

'I didn't have time to look before the dead guy woke up. I'll do it next.'

'I got the wallets from the two in the yard before Greenberg bagged them up,' Delaney said. 'Help me get them from these inside ones before Greenberg gets his crew in here.'

They put on fresh gloves and groped carefully through blood-soaked pockets. A few seconds after he started, Delaney sat back on his heels and asked her, 'You find any ID on the survivor, by the way?'

Sarah raised her head and said thoughtfully, 'No. Nothing in his pockets. I looked under his shirt—' Delaney raised his eyebrows. 'Because it was so big. It looked like the perfect place to hide something. But there was nothing – all he had was a cord, like a bungee cord but smaller around his neck, with a clasp on it. Nothing in the clasp.' He looked at her, dubious, and she shrugged and spread her hands. *If there's nothing in the clasp there's nothing in the clasp.*

The dead men in the house had new, sturdy-looking leather wallets and fresh-looking drivers' licenses. No credit cards, and something over five hundred dollars apiece.

'All cash,' Sarah said.

'Dealers,' Delaney said. 'Don't you think? Everything so fresh. This a good place to start the evidence pile?' He spread a plastic sheet and put them on it. 'We'll check them but I bet the ID's fake.'

He showed her the wallets from the bodies in the yard. Old, ragged and dirty wallets with dog-eared drivers' licenses, credits cards for gas and a few local stores, family snapshots in rundown yards, less than a hundred apiece in cash. The other contents were a few coins, some keys.

'Well, all this looks real enough,' Delaney said.

'Who would make up anything so lame?'

'I'll get Woody to run them. If they're genuine they sure don't say big-time, do they? What the hell are they doing here, bumping asses with these two pros?'

'You think they are?'

'Sure, don't you?'

'Yes. Big-time guns and ammo. The tats and earrings on Baldy, and the way Mr Brush Cut is pimped out. They get like divas, don't they?'

'Uh-huh. Let's walk the scene now, get the picture.'

'OK. You think Zimmy's calmed down enough to walk it with us?'

'I sent him back to the East Side where he belongs. Zimmy

has to process this a little before he can talk about it any more. He hates to make a mistake.'

'Well, Gross is right out there and he was number two on the scene, shall I get him?'

'Yes, let's walk it before it changes any more. Ollie, you come along, hmm?'

The ME crew was loading the two bodies out of the yard. Gloria had painted Day-Glo frames around them before they left, and their ghostly silhouettes gleamed now in the fading light.

Barney Gross came and stood beside the outline nearest the door, shaking his head. 'This guy – the tactic must have been that he was trying to look like a carpet cleaner to get in the house. Looks like he was carrying this clipboard, see?'

'So that's why these brochures are all over the place,' Delaney said. 'Makes sense.'

'Yeah. But evidently the boys inside didn't buy it, they just opened the door and started to shoot. Shot this guy full in the face and knocked him over backward.'

'He got hit in the hand, too,' Barney said. 'Did you see that, Sarah?'

'Yes. Big chunk of his hand was missing.'

'So's his weapon,' Ollie said. 'But I bet it was a Glock.'

'Why do you . . . Oh.' Delaney watched as Ollie gloved up, picked a flat piece of black plastic out of the gravel and turned it over.

'What do you know, it says Glock,' Ollie smirked, pleased to demonstrate his firearms expertise. He put the base plate of the magazine, intact except for a nick in one corner, back where he'd found it, and planted a marker by it, muttering, 'Bag it later.'

'One casing over there.' Sarah pointed. 'And hey, isn't that the spring?'

'Sure is,' Ollie said, planting more flags. 'Now where's the magazine?'

'Right there under that aloe,' Sarah said.

'Gotcha.' Another flag.

'Isn't it strange,' Barney said, 'how often people will shoot the gun instead of the person holding it?'

'I guess that muzzle pointed at you is kind of mesmerizing,' Sarah said. 'You think you're aiming at the shooter but you seize up on the little round hole.'

'And when the base plate flew off and the innards dropped out,' Ollie said, looking around, 'where do you suppose the rest of that Glock flew off to?'

'Come on, play find-the-gun later,' Delaney said. 'Let's talk about how this went down while we still got Barney here.'

They walked to the bottom of the littered yard and stood over the outline of the man who had gone so far with so many bullets in him.

'So this one gets the tough-hombre award, huh?' Sarah said.

'Probably in shock too, sometimes that helps,' Barney said. 'See all the wood chips on the gravel? Both trees in this yard are all shot to hell. Front of the house is riddled with bullets. Must've been good and noisy here for a few minutes.'

'Didn't draw much of a crowd, though – that's a break.' Delaney looked down the quiet street to where a couple of cars nosed into the police barrier, their occupants talking with the officer there. 'Who called this in?'

'The woman in that corner house across the street.' Sarah pointed. Several cars were clustered there now. 'Barry said she was crying all while she talked to him. Not surprising – over there alone with two babies, hiding with them under the bed.'

'What's her name?'

'Josephina Quintana,' Sarah said. 'Victim/witness people are there with her now.'

Back inside the house, Doctor Greenberg and his helpers were bagging the bodies against the wall. No use making any outlines here, Sarah told Delaney. 'This part of the crime scene is hopelessly muddled. We had to move them to get the ex-dead-guy out. But we've got plenty of pictures of the way things were.' She described the odd pile-up, one body on top of the other – that still bothered her. 'Didn't you think their position was hard to understand, Barney?'

'I didn't notice that,' Barney said. 'The timing is what caught my attention. This dark-haired guy that was on top, remember how he was, on his side with his hand out toward the AK47? Well, if you look at all the slugs in the door frame, and around it in the wall, you have to figure he stood right here and just sprayed. But he could only have done that after the bald guy took a blast in the belly and fell out over the step. My guess is that first shot that killed Baldy came from the big Smith & Wesson down there by the runner.'

'So Brush Cut here got shot at the same time as the guy we just sent to the hospital,' Ollie said, 'or a little after, I guess.'

'How, though?' Sarah said.

'How what?'

'How'd the third man stand behind the man with the assault rifle and get shot two seconds sooner? Which he would have to do to end up on the bottom.'

'Good question.' Delaney was chewing two or three sticks of gum methodically the way he usually did at a crime scene, like it was part of his job and he had to do it as well as he possibly could. 'But I suppose there were bullets flying all around, hmmm?' Scanning the room, blinking, he said, 'Where's his weapon, by the way?'

'Whose? Oh, the third man? I don't know, must be here somewhere.' Sarah looked under the highboy, under the chair.

'Any chance it's still on him?' He was looking at her. 'You did pat him down, didn't you, when you put him on the gurney?'

'Of course I patted him down. Best I could while we were loading – the paramedic giving me a bad time, insisting I quit fooling around so he could save the man's life.'

'Well, they're paid to hurry,' Ollie said.

'Yeah. So I had to hurry, too – but he didn't have a gun in any of the usual places. Guarantee it.'

'You check his waistband in the back?'

'Sure.'

'And his crotch, they got those damn things now—'

'Boss, he was the bottom man in a pile of bodies when I found him. Out cold. How could he put a gun in his underwear?'

'So you didn't.' He was chewing faster, staring at her.

'They were all dead, OK; I was looking at a pile of dead guys?' Sarah's voice had turned high and anxious. 'Then suddenly the bottom one was awake and all any of us could think of was getting him to a hospital fast.'

'I understand that,' Delaney said. 'But now I'm thinking about what you keep saying.'

'About what?'

'That there was something funny about his position; you can't understand how he ended up under the other man.'

'That's not all that's funny here,' Barney said, breaking in between the two tense detectives, all goodwill and muscle. 'Come on, let me show you.' He was stuck being the tour guide; he wanted to finish the tour and get back to his regular shift.

Dusky light poured in when he opened the drape on the back wall and showed Delaney the open window. They followed him outside and stood around Delaney while he frowned at the glass circles and the cutting tool. Then Barney told him about the running man he'd seen on the way here, and how he'd shot a few seconds of video and taken his photograph instead of stopping because his orders were to get here fast, officer needs assistance.

Delaney kept shaking his head and blinking. He was getting too much puzzling information all at once, Sarah saw. His mind was still on the ex-dead-guy's missing gun. This window with holes cut out of it didn't seem to fit the rest of the crime. As for the running man, she could see him thinking, *Isn't he the least of our worries?* 'You pretty sure you got his picture?'

'I got something. Might be a little blurred.'

'Take it down to the backup van and get Woody to put it up on the video screen there. See if he can clear it up enough to see what you got.'

'Now,' Delaney said when he was gone, 'Let's see what's in the garage.'

Sarah had found a key ring in the bald man's pocket, but the shiny black SUV was unlocked. Delaney walked around to the driver's door. Sarah pulled open the rear door on the passenger's side and yelped.

'*What?*' Delaney yanked his door open. They both stared, then laughed, embarrassed.

'He looked real,' Sarah said, 'for a minute.'

'What the hell?'

'It's a balloon. An inflatable man. Extra security, maybe, for the drug runs?'

'Jeez, hat and all. Yeah, with these smoked windows, I guess – Sarah, what's the matter?' She had her fists pressed hard against her temples, face screwed into a knot.

'Whether I can prove it or not, I know that man's position was wrong,' she said. 'The one we sent to the hospital? And why was he wearing gloves? Boss, I think I should call that rescue crew and tell them—'

She was still opening her phone when his rang. He said, 'Yes, Blake.' Sarah folded her phone and listened, feeling her heart constrict. Then Delaney said, '*What?*' His eyes closed to slits during a longish story that he punctuated with short questions. Sarah watched as his face turn paler and stonier.

When he folded up the phone he told her the bad news quickly. The man whose life they had tried to save had attacked the crew of the rescue vehicle and escaped. The officer-escort was in the hospital.

'I need to go talk to that officer,' Sarah said. 'Right away. Did you say his name's Fitzgerald?'

'John Fitzgerald, yes. You got your recorder? That phone take good pictures?' As usual, Delaney was concentrating on the job at hand, not wasting time with blame.

He didn't need to – Sarah felt rotten enough without a reprimand. She'd had a hand in an incident that was going to go into the record as a screw-up. First Zimmy, then her – two experienced officers had both misjudged what they were looking at. *How did he fool us like that?* Their mistake had already caused all this trouble and would almost certainly cause more down the road. For the department, maybe – that was the part that stung like a hornet. *I can take all the hard work, but I hate being wrong.*

The very last of the sunset rimmed the western mountains with crimson as she drove away from the yard. They were near enough to the south edge of town to get whiffs of the cooling desert – creosote, dust and smoke – and now that traffic had slowed she could hear mourning doves and a distant coyote. Evening brought moments of sweet repose – though not, of course, for homicide detectives who had just screwed up.

No use holding a wake over it, Delaney would say. Mistakes happen. Own up to it, deal with it, move on.

Easy for you to say. Only it wasn't – Delaney might take heat for her error in judgment; he was responsible for the job his crew turned in. *Damn.* Driving toward the hospital, her gut burned with shame. *I should never have let that Blake kid rush me.* One part of her mind was already playing the scene over, being shrewd Sarah Burke this time, saying, *Wait a minute, I need to see his underwear and get those boots off before you take him away.* Making everybody wait while she patted every inch of that little sneak down, stripped him bare. *Found his weapon* – maybe even – *is it possible that dirty little sneak got away with a pile of money too?*

No. I'd have felt—

Finally – the hospital. *Need a parking spot close to the . . . there's one.*

She badged the desk attendant, said she needed to speak to Officer Fitzgerald, asked for his room number and met the frozen indifference of a male clerk so young he thought thirty-five-year-old women were edging into their quaint phase.

'Just have a seat there, Detective,' he said, sliding a glance past her ear. 'I'll see if he can have visitors.' Sarah fixed him in a stolid stare and stood where she was, rehearsing the two quick stages by which her request would turn insistent and then threatening if this pushy upstart decided to make her wait.

Luckily he was just showing his chops, not really looking for a fight. He showed a lot more respect after he got an instant OK from the guard upstairs. She squeezed into an almost-full elevator and got an aide to help her negotiate the maze upstairs.

Fitzgerald was propped up on pillows with a big bandage on his broken nose. He had sedative in him and was getting glassy-eyed, but rallied when she asked if he could talk.

'Oh, shur.' He sounded like the first day of a massive head cold. 'Lucky to hab a dose to worry aboud.' He looked sheepish. 'Feel so dumb ledden that li'l shit ged the jump on me.'

'Join the club, John,' Sarah said. 'He fooled me, too.'

'You can call me Fitz – most people do.'

'OK, Fitz. I won't ask you to smile.' She took his picture and showed him she was pushing the start button on her recorder. He wasn't startled. Street cops recorded almost everything they did now, wary of a public that could go from please-help-me to sue-your-ass in a blink. 'Start at the beginning, will you?' she asked him. 'You left in the ambulance with the prisoner and the rescue crew—'

Fitzgerald touched his rapidly darkening eye bruises and winced. 'Yeah, the driver was floor-boarding it, we had this supposedly dying man on board. Patient's eyes were closed, he wasn't breathing that I could see. The paramedic, his name was Blake, was setting up the IV and having trouble because the vehicle sways a lot. He's kind of a perfectionist, I guess, seemed very anxious to get everything right.'

'Got kind of a high-stress job, I guess,' Sarah said.

'He should try mine. Anyway, he said help me, hold his arm like this so I can get the needle in – and I leaned over the gurney. I'm hanging onto the overhead support with one hand, see, we both are, because we're screaming around corners on one wheel . . . then like lightning, that supposedly dead guy hit me in the face with something hard.'

'How? We had him strapped on that gurney—'

'I know. And we covered him with a blanket, but Blake had pulled both his arms out, looking for the best vein for an IV . . . the weird thing is, that victim had blood all over him, he looked completely wasted, but when he went into action, holy shit he was strong. He threw me right across that gurney into Blake. Knocked him down, and he and I got wedged together in that tiny space with me on top, bleeding on him like a stuck pig from my broken nose.'

'I hope they got it set nice and straight,' Sarah said.

'Right. So I can be the straight-nosed asshole who let the prisoner get away.'

'Oh, please – I feel bad enough.'

'Why should you feel bad? You didn't have anything to do with what happened to me.'

'I let that faker fool me into thinking he was dead. Then when he seemed to wake up a little I just assumed he was terribly hurt and rushed him off to the hospital.'

'Well, for what it's worth I thought he was a goner myself. I could swear he never even breathed till he threw me into Blake.'

Fitzgerald was looking pretty gone himself. And a nurse was there with another shot, saying, 'Detective, this patient needs to rest now.'

Sarah raised one hand, fending her off. 'One minute. Fitz, tell me what happened after he attacked you. Then you can sleep.'

'He jumped off that gurney while Blake and I were still on the floor. Slid right out of those straps, slid open the little window in front and jumped into the front passenger seat. Then from what I could hear it sounded like he was pointing a gun at the driver.'

'Did you see where he got the gun from?'

'No. I never saw the gun at all but he must have had one because he told the driver, "Stop right now or I'll blow your head off." The driver's screaming, "I'm in four lanes of traffic, gimme a minute." But that crazy guy just said, "Get over right now or I'll kill you." I'm still wound around Blake, he's yelling at me to get off him – like I was lying on him for the fun of it, jeez.'

'Blake got pretty excited, huh?'

'Well, we were both a little crazy, I guess. I had so much blood in my eyes, running down my face – I never knew before what blood *tastes* like. Rusty metal, yuck. I couldn't see anything, and we were still going like a bat – I thought we were all going to die, any minute. But that driver – he really should get a medal. He kept his lights and siren going and bullied his way out of traffic and into a . . . a ramp or something—'

'Where?'

'Not sure. We'd just turned off Campbell, I think, onto Elm – we were almost to UMC. That is where I am, isn't it?'

'Yes.'

'OK, so soon as the rig stopped that nut job forced the driver out and yelled, 'Take off your shirt!' Surprised the poor driver so much he just did as he was told. And that guy I thought was all but dead, he grabbed that shirt and ran off like a deer, right through traffic! He was nowhere in sight when the driver climbed back in the cab.'

Fitz started to laugh, stopped quickly and said, 'Ow, hurts to laugh!' He touched his bandage gingerly, wincing. Then one careful snicker forced its way out. 'The driver said, "That dirty pup took my shirt!" Like *that* was the worst thing that happened!

'My face hurt so much . . . I think I yelled something. Then I passed out. I must have fallen on the floor again – my elbows hurt like hell now. When I woke up I was here. I don't know where the rescue crew is.'

'Headed back to the firehouse, telling Delaney all about it on the phone. Boy, are they happy campers now.'

'Detective,' the nurse said, 'please.'

'Nurse Bell.' Standing up, reading off her name plate, Sarah got right into Nurse Bell's pretty dimpled face and enjoyed, for three vibrating seconds, the impulse to let the whole day's shit run down on this tidy person. Threaten her with obstruction of justice, contributing to . . . something. Teach a little respect for the law in here.

Luckily some well-trained synapses fired in her brain, reminding her she had work to do and no energy to waste on folly. 'I am conducting a homicide investigation,' she said, doing her best to sound like Moses handing down stone tablets. 'The answers I'm getting are urgently needed or I wouldn't have come over here. Leave me alone and I will finish quickly.'

Nurse Bell's face froze over. She took one step back from the bed and turned to the door, her clean hands gripping the little tray with the water glass and the hypodermic in its sheath. Her expression as she walked out said, *You are on my turf now and we will see about this.*

Sarah turned back to Fitz, who drooped on his pillows, too wasted to take any interest in another fight. 'You passed out before you had time to phone in a BOLO, is that right?'

'But somebody did, I guess,' Fitz said, 'because you're here.'

Finished or not, she was going to have to stop; he was falling asleep. 'Can you remember anything about his appearance?'

'I just got on my feet as he jumped out of the truck.' Fitz's head wobbled. Eyes half closed, he said, 'He wasn't as big as I expected.' His chin dropped on his chest. Then, with one final heroic effort he lifted his head and added: 'He was wearing surgical gloves!'

'Here's my card.' She put it on the bedside table. 'When you wake up, Fitz, if you think of anything more, call me.' In case he was not as comatose as he looked, she added: 'Don't worry about this incident. You got handed a rotten mess, and you did the best anybody could do with it. I'll put that in my report. Sleep now.'

Just saying the word made her long to lie down on the hard tile floor beside his bed and grab some Zs for herself.

Don't even think about it.

She hurried out into the hall, nodding pleasantly as she passed Nurse Bell, who was headed toward the doorway with a doctor in tow.

Outside in cooling darkness, she drove back to the Midvale Park neighborhood talking to her buddy Kate, who was running the shift at the West Side Station.

'Delaney called about the escape,' Kate said. 'We're setting up the containment area now. Eight blocks each way around UMC – we're getting help from Midtown since the hospital's in their division. Two K-9 units are on their way; they'll walk grids in the area. Sergeant Holly's supervising, and the gang unit from Midtown's coming over, too. You got anything more for a physical description?'

'Dark hair, pale eyes. Maybe five-nine. Strong but not large. Wearing a dark blue collared polo shirt with the firehouse logo on the back.'

'What?'

'Yeah, he took it off the driver, how's that for cool? This guy's quick and resourceful. Armed and very dangerous. Tell everybody, he's . . .' She took a breath, trying to think how to convey the threat. 'He has some tricks I've never seen before.'

'Like what?'

'Like, he knows how to control his pulse and breathing. He can play dead.'

'Come on.'

'I wouldn't believe it if I hadn't seen it, Kate. Zimmy declared him dead at the scene and I fully agreed with his judgment. But just now he threw an able-bodied officer right across a gurney that he himself was lying full length on – strapped to it, actually.'

'Whoa. Houdini's come back?'

'Or something. Pass the word to everybody on shift tonight, 'Look around you every minute. Trust no one. A clever killer is on the loose.'

FIVE

Robin had no plan at all when he jumped out of the van. He just knew he didn't want to be strapped to a gurney under guard, so he took the first chance he got to escape.

He had no idea where he was. *Just get out of the van*, his instincts told him, *and then deal with whatever comes next*. Quick reaction times, he knew, were his major asset.

He had a good eye for foraging, too. Most people in the middle of an emergency entrance, people yelling all around and horns and sirens sounding, might see a guy with a clean shirt and wish they had it but think there was no time for that. Robin made time, almost literally – by not hesitating, he created little pockets of time that most people didn't have. When he saw something he wanted, if nobody stopped him he took it right away. He had been hurt a few times while he learned how fast you had to be, but the reward was worth it – he often threw people off balance by the audacity with which he put his own desires ahead of everything.

The cop whose face he'd smashed was yelling something in the van. It sounded garbled – he must be choking on his own blood. He hadn't followed them out yet so he probably wasn't coming at all. With no cop to worry about and the driver climbing back into his seat, Robin stood still and pulled off his bloody shirt. He started to drop it right there, but then he heard that doctor in the rescue van begin yelling for help on the radio. So now a lot of people were going to be looking for the missing patient, right here. Better if they didn't find a bloody shirt in this entrance.

He rolled the shirt up and got ready to toss it into a big garbage receiver beside the emergency entrance. At the last second he remembered the little radio in the sleeve. He pulled it out and stuck it in his pants pocket, giddy at the thought of how close he'd come to forgetting his favorite small device. He used it all the time, loved it because it kept him in touch

with the world but didn't leave a trail or need to be plugged
in. Secretly, to himself only, he called it 'Little Brother.'

There, the bloody shirt was out of sight.

He still didn't know where he was going. The street was
full of crazy traffic and offered no cover. There were small
bushes and cacti all around this driveway but they wouldn't
hide him for more than a minute. The van he'd jumped out
of was beginning to move into the building under the emergency sign, so he couldn't go there. He pulled on the clean
shirt and walked around the building, toward the front.

He knew he had blood on his pants but they were dark.
Indoors out of the sun, the stains probably wouldn't show.

Nobody stopped him on the steps. He took a deep breath
and opened the front door. *Look as if you know what you're
doing.*

Inside was a lobby with a long desk. There were many
people – all too busy to look at him, good. He saw a sign that
said, 'Restrooms,' and walked toward it briskly, eyes straight
ahead. Inside the men's room, he used the urinal and cleaned
up at the farthest sink from the door, using wet paper towels
so the blood wouldn't show in the sink. Another good thing:
men were mostly uneasy in public toilets these days, not
wanting to look at each other. Several came and went, paying
no attention to him.

When he came out he walked past the desk to the elevators,
got in the first one that opened and rode to the third floor –
high enough to see his surroundings, not too far to run down
if something spooked him. He didn't know the building and
was basically surfing. But he found the first thing he wanted
quickly, a service desk where people in scrubs came and went
and patients' charts were stacked in a rack. He set an oblique
course for it, slowing down while two aides conferred there,
speeding up when they walked away. As he walked past the
desk he picked a chart off the rack and walked straight on to
a door marked, 'Stairs.'

Climbing to the fourth floor, he felt his confidence soar. He
was doing very well, wearing a dark blue uniform shirt that
said he worked for the Tucson Fire Department, and carrying
a chart he could look down at and appear to study. That was

cover enough to allow him to walk these halls till he decided where to go next. He could even stand still for a couple of minutes, pretending to look at the chart while he checked the view outside the windows. So far, he was pleased about what he was not seeing – no squads of armed men in black vests climbing out of vehicles, no blue uniforms leashed to ominously poised dogs. He knew they would be looking for him soon. But they weren't here yet.

Halfway through his circuit of the building he found himself looking out of a huge bank of windows facing west. Across an adjoining parking lot was a large light-colored building with a sign that read, 'Children's Hospital.' Behind it, connected by a couple of ramps was a four-story parking garage, big enough so a clever guy with the right shirt and a chart for cover should be able to hide there for a long time. He could stay in the shadows . . . move from one floor to another if it looked as if somebody was starting to notice him. But who looks at anybody in a parking garage, unless he's doing something strange?

Since he got out of prison, Robin had made almost an art of looking completely nondescript. He kept his hair short, stayed slim and never wore anything strange or noteworthy. He walked quietly now, keeping his eyes on the floor a few paces ahead. In his mind he was fading into the walls – he was hardly there at all.

With no hesitation, he turned back toward the sign for the stairs, reviewing the advantages of his new hideout. That parking ramp had access to two huge buildings where people came and went at all hours. They would give him cover when he wanted to move. He'd have a choice of restrooms, plenty of vending machines holding food and drinks. Unless a dog flushed him – he'd have to think about that – he could stay in this complex as long as he needed to.

Following signs that said, 'TO PARKING,' he made his way toward the ramps that led to the garage. This was the hard part, where he was pretty exposed, so he had to do it right away before the search for him got organized. It helped that everybody in this complex was very busy – many looked at their watches as they walked. In a few minutes, he was out of the sun-drenched open spaces between the hospitals and walking into the shadows of the parking garage.

Now all he had to do when anybody came near him was look as if he was looking for a car. Which in fact he would be, pretty soon, he thought with growing pleasure. In a day or two, as soon as all those cops cleared out of the house on Spring Brook Drive, he would start to decide which car he wanted to boost out of this garage. No hurry about it, though. He could decide that fast enough, when he was ready to go back and get the money.

SIX

'The narc squad came and took away a truckload of marijuana,' Delaney said, 'and that bag of coke and the pipes out of the kitchen.' He was standing in the middle of the front yard, eerily lit by halogen lamps, when Sarah ducked under the tape. He had his phone in one hand and his radio in the other, and seemed to have a conversation going on both. 'They didn't find any money, though.'

'They searched the whole house while I was gone?'

'No, just the room the dope was in. I asked them not to search the rest of the house because the lab crew was still working inside.'

'So now it's up to us to find it?'

'If there's any here. The runaway couldn't have had it on him, could he? You'd have found it.'

'Yes, I'd have found it.' She said it firmly to hide the little wobble of uncertainty she felt. How could you be entirely sure of anything with a man who had changed from victim to suspect, dead one minute and alive the next? 'Greenberg's gone with the bodies too, huh? Did he say when he might do the autopsies?'

'Said he'd have to let us know. My crew's all here, finally – all but Tobin. I forgot his vacation starts tomorrow. I guess he left early.'

Or you didn't have the heart to tell him to stop packing and get over here.

'So I gave the scene to Jason.' Across the yard, she could see Jason Peete's shaved head gleaming in the light from the front door. He was bent over the plastic bucket with the bullet hole. 'Ray's down the block talking to the woman who called this in. She wouldn't talk to anybody else, but he dredged up a few Spanish words and persuaded her he was harmless.'

'Helps if your name's Menendez, huh? I'd like to hear what she has to say, but I'd better not interrupt.'

'No. Ray'll have a recording. Is Fitz OK?'

'I think so.' She told him the story of the attack and escape.

'That's about what I got from the rescue squad.'

'Except they don't feel any remorse – it's not their job to keep anybody on board if he wants to leave. But poor Fitz is giving himself grief about letting a prisoner escape.'

'Well, the firemen were giving *me* grief – bad enough we got turned away and called back, they said, but then the guy we're supposed to be saving attacks us. They wanted to know, what kind of police can't tell dead from alive?'

'Listen, Zimmy and I are the same kind of police we were yesterday – we just ran into a corpse with unusual attributes.'

'"A corpse with unusual attributes."' Delaney looked pleased. 'That's pretty good, Sarah – may I quote you?'

'Sure. I called Kate, gave her a physical description and told her about the surgical gloves.'

'Did she get the containment put together fast enough to do any good?'

'Maybe. She got great help from everybody . . . but he's fast, and there're plenty of places around the university he can go to ground.' She wiped her dry mouth. 'I have to find some water.'

'In front of the backup van, just outside the tape there. Soon as you have a drink will you see how Oscar's doing? He's going through that carpet cleaners' van in the driveway. I told him, figure out if it's part of the crime scene. If it's not we'll get it towed out of here.'

'The techs have finished with it?'

'Yes. Go on, get some water, you're starting to wilt.'

She ducked under the tape, feeling her knees wobble as she straightened up. She really was dehydrated – damn, it happened fast sometimes when you were rushed in hot weather. She fished a bottle out of the ice in a cooler on the gravel, then climbed inside the trailer and perched on a stool to drink. Cool water running down her throat felt like the correct answer to all the trouble in the universe. She took another gulp, sighed, closed her eyes and felt her molecules expand. *Oh, man. More like it.*

When she opened her eyes she was looking at the back of

a criminalist sitting at a console, surrounded by wires and electronics. 'Hey, Woody.' The screen beyond him showed a continuous loop of a running man. 'Is that Barney's video?'

'Yup.'

'Pretty good picture.'

'Not bad. Ever see that guy?'

'Don't think so.' She squinted. 'Shee. Rainbow-colored tats, huh? And an eyebrow ring.'

'And a Justin Bieber haircut. Quite a dude.'

The loop started over at the beginning, the runner looking around frantically at the sound of the siren. 'Is that a pistol in his belt?'

'Looks like it. Guess I'll copy a couple of frames, send them down to ballistics. They might be able to ID the weapon.'

'I should think so, yeah.' She drained the last of her water. 'I'm taking one of these for the road. I got too dry back there for a few minutes, almost turned into part of the desert.'

'Yeah, you gotta be careful the first couple of weeks of summer. The heat can kill you while you're thinking about other things.'

Getting up off the stool, she felt fatigue cramp all her muscles. She told her feet to quit complaining and carry her out to the cooler. They gimped a little, but they made it. The ice made a nice slithery tinkle when she pulled another water bottle out. She set the bottle down, scooped up a double handful of ice and buried her face in it. When it started to burn she dropped it on the gravel and let the air dry her skin.

Aaahh! Good to go again. She uncapped the second bottle, enjoyed another cold swallow, and shook herself. Feeling her cramped muscles loosen up, she looked across the lot at the dingy old Ford cargo van in the driveway. Least interesting vehicle I've seen this week, she decided, and walked toward it, wondering, *Now, what will Officer Studly have found fascinating about this heap that I would never notice?*

When Oscar Cifuentes joined the homicide squad last year, he had been preceded by a reputation as a tireless womanizer whose other major interest was auto mechanics. Sarah thought the first was pitiful and the second boring, so for the first couple of months she was polite but cool toward the new detective. But when a case erupted into a crisis involving a vintage car, Cifuentes showed her he could be quick and enterprising, and was profoundly knowledgeable about rolling stock. Now that they'd worked a few cases together, they were practically buds. No chemistry, that was part of it – it was somehow clear from the start that he was never going to try any of his Mr Irresistible moves on her. And she liked the patient way he picked at a puzzle till he unraveled it.

The sign on the side of the van read, 'Bestway Carpet Cleaners.' A glance inside the open rear doors confirmed that the cargo space was filled with industrial-size vacuums and scrubbers. *I suppose he's already noted the tool marks on the license plate.*

Cifuentes sat in the open passenger doorway, reading. When she walked up beside him he looked up and said, 'Doesn't look abandoned. The registration's in the glove compartment.'

'Valid, you think?'

'Matches the model number and the VIN.'

'But not the license plate, I bet.'

'Oh? Haven't got that far.' He climbed out, carrying the form, and walked back. 'Bingo. Oh, you spotted the tool marks, huh?' He smiled. 'Thought you said you didn't give a damn about cars.'

'I don't. But I put in my year and something in auto theft.'

'Oh, right.' They stood together by the open rear doors, looking in at the jumble of equipment. 'What's your impression of the cleaning gear?'

'Well used but still in working order.'

'That's what I thought.' He tapped his lip. 'So, a working cargo van, recently stolen from—' He looked at the slip. 'Edward Benson, up in Oracle. This the new trend for thugs? Swipe a service truck to do the dirty deed?'

'Or Benson's one of the bodies in the yard?'

'Don't think so – this van was boosted. The ignition is spun.'

'Ah. You checked the reports yet?'

'No. I just found this.'

'If Benson's a small business owner who just lost his cargo van, he'd report the theft right away.'

'Yes, he would.' He pulled out his keys, jingled them once in his hand, thinking, then stuck them back in his pocket and said, 'My car and laptop's way down at the other end of the block. I'm going to take this over to Woody and let him type it in.'

'Fine.' She walked along with him. 'Did the techs find anything interesting on this vehicle?'

'They took candy wrappers downtown to check for prints. One promising lift on the passenger door, Gloria said. DNA later, maybe.' They both shrugged. DNA would help lawyers in court, way down the line, if they were all lucky. Right now, a killer was on the loose in Tucson. They couldn't wait for DNA.

'The fact that the VIN wasn't changed,' Sarah said, 'and the registration was still in the van . . . if Benson's not in on the caper, what does that tell you?'

'Vehicle was probably snatched off the street earlier today, just for this job. They intended to ditch it right away, so they didn't bother being thorough.'

'Yeah. Quick and dirty. Let me know about Benson, will you? I gotta go see how Ollie's doing with the guns and ammo.'

Oscar laughed. 'He's had two guys helping him cut sections out of drywall and siding for over an hour. This house is going to look like a lace doily by the time he's done.'

'I'm never going to be done.' Peering up from the baseboard where he crouched, his Leatherman drooping from his limp hand, Ollie crossed his eyes and let his tongue hang out. 'My destiny is to continue cutting careful sections out of this stinking house until my right hand breaks off at the wrist.'

'Oh, and I suppose when it does,' Sarah said, 'you'll start whining about needing a doctor.' Ice-water was percolating through her tissues, doing wonders for her sense of humor. 'How many slugs have you collected so far?'

'They're stacked on the kitchen table; take a look.'

'Shee,' she said, looking at the table. 'You did all this while I was gone?'

'Me and my team. Delaney got me two helpers out of city

maintenance when he had to put Jason on the scene. See those
two guys out there in jumpsuits? They're digging the last slugs
out of the trees.'

The guns were all there on the table too, ranged on a soft
cloth at one end, waiting for Ollie to disarm them before
bagging and tagging.

'Hey, you found the Glock.' It lay on the table, beside its
magazine, baseplate and spring, the pieces side by side on the
towel.

'By accident, after I quit looking. I went out in the yard to
get my helpers started, turned on my flashlight, and it shined
right on the Glock. It was up in the crotch of that palo verde
tree. I guarantee I could not get it to hang there on purpose
if I tried all day.'

At the other end of the table, heaps were taking shape –
squares of drywall in one pile, outdoor siding in another,
clumps of tree bark in a third. Each section had a slug in its
center and was bagged in clear plastic. Each bag carried a tag
describing the exact location where it was found. Ollie
Greenaway's team did neat, careful work.

'You found anything yet that doesn't look like it could have
come from the guns you've got here?'

'No. But that's very preliminary. Why?'

'Well, somebody had to fire the last shot. From the position
of the bodies and the weapons it looks like it must have been
Mr Brush Cut. But then who killed him?'

'Ah, Sarah, leave that for the lab. We do all this collecting;
the least they can do is carry the water from there.'

Jason stuck his head in the open front door and said, 'Sarah,
somebody's waiting for you down by the tape line.'

'Oh?' She walked over and he pointed. Will Dietz was
standing there with his arms full. She ran down, smiling.
'Brought you some snacks,' he said, passing the sacks. 'Careful,
this one's coffee.'

'You are a prince among men,' she said, 'and I will thank
you appropriately at a later time.'

'When you get your strength back.' He gave her the half-
wink that passed for terms of endearment during working
hours. 'How's your long day going?'

'It's a big mess. We'll be here a while yet.' As he turned to go she asked him, 'You heard anything on the containment?'

'Just that there is one. They after somebody you want?'

'Yeah. He's a bad one, Will, watch your back tonight.'

'Always do.' He got into the driver's side of his vehicle and rode away with his face set in its standard street-cop expression: No Big Deal. Watching him go, she felt lucky and, momentarily, not at all tired.

She pulled a warm apple Danish out of a sack, walked back into the busy crime scene house and ate it leaning against a kitchen counter. She had been appalled the first time she watched crime scene detectives ordering in pizza at a crime scene. But she was a seasoned homicide detective now and accepted that the hard mental work of an investigation burned through calories like wildfire and made her ravenous. So she relished the good pastry and fresh coffee, ignoring the bloody crime scene all around her. When she was done she went back to work with fresh energy.

Delaney, his face like an overwound clock, walked into the house and asked Ollie, 'You found the Glock yet?'

'Yeah, it's there on the table.'

'And you got all the rest of the weapons sequestered in here, right? Have you disarmed them yet?'

'No. I want to list them first, with the ammo just as I found them. When we start diagraming how this all went down, the bullet count might make a lot of difference.'

'I guess that's right,' Delaney said. 'But why don't you do that next so we can get the weapons bagged and tagged?' He frowned at the neat array on the table. 'I don't like them lying around like this with everybody walking through. If you step out – we've got people working here now that aren't even sworn.'

Ollie's face froze into a craggy slope of freckled rock. The usually cheery clown morphed into a proud detective with twenty years' experience, unaccustomed to having his work criticized. Oblivious to the anger he was leaving behind him, Delaney, frowning and thinking so hard he forgot to chew his gum, stomped out over the bloody doorsill.

'Go shit a brick, Sergeant,' Ollie said softly behind him.

'Whose idea was it to bring in the extra crew?' He'd waited till Delaney was out of earshot though, Sarah noticed. Proud or not, he was still too mindful of his mortgage to get in a pissing match with his boss.

'Listen, don't waste your energy getting mad,' Sarah said. 'We've still got a lot of miles to—' She stopped, staring out the door.

'What?' Ollie said. 'You see something?' But she had already bolted out the door, calling, 'Boss?' because she had just remembered what she should do next.

Delaney didn't hear her and kept right on walking. Not willing to scream at a crime scene, she broke into a fast trot and caught him just before he reached the tape. When she was directly behind him she took a deep breath and said quietly, 'Sergeant?'

He whirled, bug-eyed, and said, '*What?*'

'Sorry.' She gave him a minute to recover before she said, 'The shirt.'

'What shirt?' Back to his stony calm, he stared past her left ear, concentrating on some info nexus in the middle distance while she told him about the shirt stolen from the firehouse driver. 'Fitz said he changed right there in the street,' she said. 'Chances are he just dropped the bloody shirt and left it there.'

'Might have. Did Fitzgerald say where they were when this happened?'

'He couldn't remember exactly – somewhere near the hospital. But the driver should know.'

'You know the driver's name?'

'No. But somebody at the fire station ought to.'

'Which station?'

'I don't know. But what use is it being a detective if I can't find that out? OK if I—'

'Sure, go for it.'

She called 911, got the attendant who answered the phone to read his dispatch sheet and tell her he'd sent the rescue squad from Fire Station Eighteen to the house on Spring Brook Drive tonight.

'Twice tonight, actually.'

'Um, yes. We thought we didn't need them, then we did.

Now I need to find that driver again. So may I have that number, please?'

The phone rang twice at the firehouse before a brisk female voice said, 'This is Sergeant Graves.'

'This is Detective Sarah Burke, Sergeant. Are you in charge of the shift?'

'Yes, I am.'

'So was it you who sent the emergency rescue truck to the house in Midvale Park tonight?'

'Yes. Twice, actually.'

'Yeah, we're really sorry about that. There was a . . . mmm . . . little mix-up about the first call. And then, the second time, there was an incident—'

'Is that what you call it, an incident? Maury said he almost got his head blown off.'

'Yeah. I'm sorry about that, too. But – Maury was the driver when the prisoner got away?'

'Yes.'

'I need to speak to him.'

'Well . . . he's on break right now.'

The firehouse crews worked twenty-four-hour shifts, Sarah knew, and Maury's 'break' meant he was getting some shuteye in his cubicle after his wild ride. *But I need that shirt.* She tuned up her Moses voice again and said, 'Well, then I'm sorry for the third time, but I'm a homicide detective on the trail of a very bad guy, so let me speak to him now, please.'

There was a moment of dead silence while Sergeant Graves, presumably, took a deep breath. Then her calm, sensible voice said, 'Hold on.'

Maury Mangen's phone rang three times before he answered, sounding sleepy. Not wasting any more time on sorry, Sarah identified herself and said, 'I need to know where you were when the man you were transporting took your shirt.'

'Uh . . .' She listened while he breathed. 'I was on Campbell, a couple of blocks south of the hospital. In four lanes of traffic, doing fifty in a thirty-five zone, when he stuck that gun in my ear and told me to stop the truck. I had the siren going, and in another block I'd fought my way into the turn lane for the hospital, so I stopped.'

'And got out of the van?'

'Sure. Wouldn't you, if a guy put a gun in your ear and told you to? And that crazy fool came right out behind me and told me to take off my shirt.'

'Did he drop his own shirt when he took it off?'

'Did he what?'

'Did he drop the bloody shirt he took off right there?'

'Hell, I don't know. Cars were honking, the cop in the back of the ambulance was yelling . . . last I saw of the crazy patient he was walking around the corner toward the front of the hospital, pulling on my shirt. I don't think he had anything in his hands . . . but right then the cop fainted and Blake started screaming at me to drive on – Blake's favorite answer to any problem, scream at somebody. I drove on to the emergency entrance and helped unload the bloody cop. And everybody kept asking me, 'Why are you working without a shirt?''

'So that shirt might be right there near the emergency entrance somewhere?

'Could be, for all I know.'

Nearby, a bell began to ring insistently. Sergeant Graves called something through an echoing PA system.

'OK, Maury,' Sarah said. 'Thanks, I'll let you get back to your nap.'

'Yeah, well, the way it sounds right now,' Maury said grimly, 'it's going to be a while before anybody does any more napping around here.'

Feeling guilty and triumphant by turns, Sarah went outside, found Delaney and asked his permission to go look for the shirt.

'That's not best use of your time,' he said. 'Call Midtown and have them send a uniform to look for it. I was just coming to find you. They called off the containment – the guy got away.'

'Damn.'

'Yeah. So now I'm thinking . . . so far as we know, we don't have anything yet that will help us ID that guy, do we?'

'No. He's got his weapon with him. He was wearing gloves – we may not have any prints. There might be some of his DNA on the floor—'

'But he was lying under the one you call Brush Cut, whose blood was all over him – that's going to take some time to sort out.'

'You look like you're thinking of something.'

'The rescue truck – especially the gurney. If it hasn't been cleaned up yet—'

'Oh, crap,' Sarah said, 'I have to call that firehouse again? But yes, OK, that's a good idea,' she said, already dialing.

The sergeant's voice was not cordial after she heard who was calling. 'What do you need, Detective?'

'Sergeant, is the small rescue truck in the station right now?'

'Uh, yeah. Maybe not for long, though. Everything else went out on that last fire call.'

With her voice crackling with stress, Sarah explained that the escaped suspect had left no fingerprints, nothing that identified him, and that he was loose in Tucson right now. 'So we were hoping . . . is it possible the gurney cover hasn't been changed yet?'

'I took it off myself and put on a clean one. Tell you what, though' – the shift commander was warming up a little, getting engaged in the problem – 'this place has been so crazy busy tonight, maybe— Hold on a minute.' There was some thumping, some murmuring. Then Sergeant Graves was back, saying, 'Well, that was lucky.'

'What?'

'I set the used cover down on a bench till I got the clean one put on, and then, so many interruptions . . . I never put it in the laundry sack.'

'Sergeant,' Sarah said, 'that's not just lucky, that's beautiful. And the truck is still there, right?' She was thinking about the escapee climbing in the front seat, sliding out the driver's door . . . gloves or no gloves, he had to leave some sweat behind.

The sergeant was very reluctant, though, to put the small rescue vehicle out of service for the rest of the night. 'What if we get another emergency? I need wheels!'

'Sergeant, I think we just encountered a problem for guys above our pay grade,' Sarah said. 'Let's see, what time is it? Almost two.' She thought for a few seconds. 'Well, it's too damn bad, but looks like we're going to have to wake some people up.' She ran and found Delaney.

'Yeah, I'll call the night shift commander,' Delaney said. 'He can shuffle some equipment around. While I do that, you call the crime lab, tell them to wake up a DNA specialist if they don't have one working. Tell them a killer's on the loose, and we need a twenty-four-hour emergency run on whatever they can get off that gurney cover and the front seat of the truck.' As she started to open her phone he added: 'Tell her to call me if there's any problem getting that started. We need results ASAP!'

He was chewing gum like a mechanical alligator and his cheeks had relaxed. 'You look as if something good happened,' Sarah said.

'Yeah, finally. Soon as you make your phone calls, come on to the backup van,' he said, heading toward it. 'Woody's got an answer back on the two wallets we found in the yard.'

SEVEN

In the backup van, Woody had pulled the records up. All the detectives were coming in from the yard. Sarah stuck her head in between Jason and Ray, trying to see the screen, and they let her squeeze through to the front since she was shorter.

The mugshot showed a white male about thirty years old with thick hair growing low on his forehead, a mean mouth and turned-off eyes. The satiny gray drape of the Pima County detention system covered his shoulders.

Jason said, 'That's the guy by the door, isn't it?'

'Yeah, Clipboard Man,' Sarah said.

'Earl LeRoy Klutzbach,' Delaney said. 'Anybody know him?' They all said no. 'This was the man nearest the house, right? We think he had the Glock?'

'Stands to reason,' Jason said. 'Pieces of it lying on the gravel, about six inches from his hand. Ollie find the rest of it yet?'

'Yes. Where is Ollie? Still in the house?' Delaney stepped outside and asked a uniform to fetch him, came back in and said, 'OK, Woody, let's scroll down to the arrest record.' It came up and they stood silent, reading.

'Well, that's odd,' Jason said. 'Just one arrest?'

'One is plenty,' Ray Menendez said, 'when it's aggravated assault.'

'But with no previous arrests? I wonder what set him off,' Jason said.

'Somebody fooled with his wife . . . or girlfriend? I remember some stuff about that case now . . . let me think.' Delaney poked three fingers into a patch of skin between his eyebrows, trying to pull the memory out of there. 'He wasn't my collar – he was arrested out in the county, in a wildcat cluster west of Marana. But the crime happened in Tucson so we got the case, and that's what I remember, the courtroom and his conviction. By the time of the trial the woman had been in therapy for a long time and she was still so terrified of being in the same room with him; she wept most of the time she was on the stand. The man she was diddling with, last I knew he still couldn't walk right.'

'Earl's been safely off the street ever since,' Ray said. 'See? Right out there in Wilmot all this time – almost twelve years.'

'Too bad he got out. What, six weeks ago? Didn't take him long to stir up more trouble. Let's see the other one, Woody.' Delaney turned and nodded at Ollie, who climbed into the already-crowded space and peered over shoulders at the screen.

A similar but much uglier face appeared there, broken-nosed and scarred, with a vacant expression. 'Same mouth and hairline,' Delaney said. 'Oh, these two are brothers.' The name under the second mugshot was Homer Evan Klutzbach.

'I know this guy,' Ollie said. 'Hell, you all know this guy, don't you? Every cop in town's arrested him one time or another.'

'I never did,' Sarah said.

Ray said, 'Is this the guy with the weird laugh? One funny eye?'

'And he rambled, right?' Jason said. 'Never gave a straight answer?'

'That's the one,' Ollie said.

Delaney said, 'You know him so well, how come none of you ID'd him out there in the yard?'

'He had about a dozen holes in him,' Jason said, 'and he was lying on what was left of his face.'

'I feel kind of disadvantaged,' Sarah said. 'I mean, how did I miss Homer? His whole record's local. What's he got there, fifteen, sixteen arrests?'

'And every time you brought him in,' Ollie said, 'you had to spell that miserable name. I bet I can still do it.' He turned his back to the screen and spelled Klutzbach, eliciting low whistles of admiration. He made a little mock bow and shrugged it off, but then couldn't quit talking about it. 'It's kind of a grabber, actually. Klutzbach. You can imagine how kids in school probably teased him . . . called him Klutzy.'

All the other detectives nodded. 'I kind of like hard names; once you learn them they're easier to remember.'

'OK, we like his name, what else?' Delaney said, impatient. 'Why only five convictions, I wonder?'

'Well, he was the kind of a guy that leads naturally to sloppy police work,' Ollie said. 'It was such a pain to have him in the car with you that you'd do anything to get him out of there and go back to talking to actual humans.'

'Man, he made full use of our facilities, didn't he?' Ray said. 'Starting with that little stretch in juvie way back in '98, he's been in almost every lockup. Eight months in Pima County, and since then he's been to Florence and Yuma and back to Florence . . . just got out of there three weeks ago. Short liberty.'

'Most of his arrests had something to do with auto theft,' Ray said. 'And the last two convictions were for carjacking. Are you sure you don't recognize him, Oscar?'

'I usually remember the cars better than the thieves,' Cifuentes said. 'Maybe if I saw an earlier photo. He looks as if he's recently put on weight.'

'That's State Prison for you. They don't exercise enough and the food is all that prefab crap. Most of the guards look the same way.'

'He had to know all the local mopes,' Delaney said. 'Get in touch with all your snitches tomorrow, find out what they know about this invasion. There must be gossip on the street – there always is.'

'I wonder what induced him to try hitting on a stash house?' Ray said. 'Seems a little upmarket for Homer.'

'Maybe just following his brother the wife-beater,' Oscar said.

'Or maybe they were both following the ex-dead-guy,' Sarah said. She blinked a couple of times and asked, 'Did the lights just go dim for a second?'

'No,' Delaney said. 'You're just getting exhausted. We all are, but we better make one organized effort to find the money before the boarding-up crew get here.'

He assigned a room to each detective while he took the garage. 'You're looking for something heavy and secure,' he said. 'A safe or a money box.'

Sarah looked around, assessing the job. 'Lucky thing, it's all tile floors and no carpet.'

'Or wallpaper,' he said. 'So let's get to it. Everything's fair game.'

They put on fresh gloves and tore the place apart. It was fun in a way, after a long day of being so careful with everything. Ray and Jason took out all the drawers in the bedrooms and studied the undersides, threw everything out of the closets and moved the beds. Ollie made a real mess out of pans and dishes in the kitchen, dismantled the stove, moved the refrigerator out and said, 'Damned if I'm sweeping *that* up.'

Sarah, in the living room, tipped over all the chairs, emptied the drawers in the console and swept everything out of a bookcase. It was full of ammo boxes, papers for joints, scissors, a couple of roaches and two bags of size nine white cotton socks, but no books. Finally she tore down the drapes. There was one Velcroed pocket built into the bottom seam of the drape on the front window. It looked like it had held a secret stash of something once but it was empty now. She was holding it open, sighing over it, when her eyes were caught by a round oak table in a corner near the kitchen door.

'Ollie,' she said, 'see that table?'

'Dining-room table. What about it?'

'Why's it crammed into a corner? Funny place to eat. Help me tip it over, will you?' It had a fat pedestal base and was heavy. As soon as they laid it on its side they both said, 'Hah!'

Ollie stuck his head out the door to the garage and said, 'Boss? Think we found something.' Delaney came in and stood with them, looking down at a trapdoor.

'Well, now,' he said, 'isn't that a pretty sight?' It had a steel ring countersunk near one edge. Ollie brought a kitchen knife and lifted it out of its groove. Delaney hooked one finger in it and lifted. The other detectives were all in the room now and as the door came up Sarah heard them all make the same sound, 'Aahh.'

'Regulation steel safe,' Delaney said. 'Nice work, guys.'

Jason said, 'Probably chock full of money, huh?' All the tired faces in the room were wearing a new expression, Sarah saw – engaged. *Nothing like money to wake everybody up.* Even though it wasn't theirs, they all wanted to see it.

'Looks like a standard Rotary lock. Going to take an expert to crack it, I guess, unless we find a combination in that laptop we sent to the lab.'

'Not to mention how freakin' hard it's going to be to pull it up out of there,' Jason said. 'Unless – did you try it?'

'What? No.' Delaney looked irritated. 'Why would anybody—' He bent and turned the handle, gave a little grunt of surprise, and lifted. The door opened wide without a squeak. Jason crowed happily.

They all looked into the dark, funky-smelling interior. An odd kind of silence fell, in which Sarah thought she could hear everybody breathe. Finally Delaney said, 'Nice and neat, isn't it? All counted and banded. Wow, it's a lot.'

'Anybody want to guess how much?' Ray said.

'A down payment on a nice house,' Sarah said.

'Or one Mercedes,' Oscar said.

'Oh, at least,' Ray said. 'Maybe enough over for an ATV.' He turned to his team-mates, looking indignant. 'Ain't that a hole in the boat, when you think about it? They make all this money and leave us all the work.'

'Earth to Ray,' Ollie said. 'They're all dead and we're alive.'

'Well, yeah, there is some risk involved,' Ray said, and they all laughed. They stopped quickly because, at their level of fatigue, laughter was dangerously close to tears.

'How do we handle it?' Sarah said, looking at Delaney.

'You mean, have I got a special sack I carry around in case I find a great deal of money?' Even Delaney had had his sense of humor revived. 'No. Just hand me a couple of the large evidence bags off that pile in the kitchen. And we better bag it in a hurry, because I hear the boarding-up crew arriving.'

'Just in time, too,' Jason said. 'I can't feel my feet any more.'

EIGHT

When his bladder woke him Zeb tiptoed silently to the bathroom and closed the door with painstaking care, grateful the hinges didn't squeak. He rinsed his hands under minimum tap water, whispered a curse when he realized he'd forgotten his towel, and dried them on his pants.

But he noticed, when he came out, that Janet's bedroom door still stood open. He took a chance and peeked. She wasn't in bed. He turned on the light to be sure. What time was it? Her bedside alarm said 3:15 a.m. Caring less and less about quiet, he looked in the living room and kitchen. When he found both rooms empty he opened the door and checked out her parking space in the lot. Her car wasn't there.

Sudden, unreasoning anger shook him. Here he was, creeping around shoeless in the dark in an empty apartment, while his sister slept over with a friend – a lover? He couldn't imagine her humorless face and angular body in bed with a man. But she was in bed somewhere, doing as she pleased, while he— Damn, why did other people have all the fun? OK, she'd never invited him to stay here – still, would it kill her to leave a note?

But no, she never gave him a thought – as usual, she acted like he wasn't even there. His anger began making a case for helping himself.

As soon as he was fully awake his gut had begun growling with hunger. Nothing but breakfast yesterday and it had been a screaming bitch of a day, all that fear and running. Crackers and a few raisins last night – what a joke! He needed real food.

It felt good to walk into the kitchen, turn on all the lights and find a frying pan. She didn't have any bacon, wouldn't you know? But plenty of eggs, and there was butter. He found bread, too, and toasted four slices while he scrambled half a

dozen eggs in a bowl. Poured them onto sizzling butter in the
pan and put two slices of cheese on top. By the time he spooned
the soft-scrambled eggs over the toast he was salivating. He
ate the whole thing as fast as he could, whimpering with
pleasure at first and then steadily stuffing the last of it down.

He had time, he reasoned: an hour at least before he had
to clean up. Might as well check the TV. Anything else here
for a treat while he watched? He found one beer at the back
of the top shelf in the refrigerator. Opened it, sat in the only
easy chair in the living room – Janet sure lived stingy, he
thought – and used the remote to turn on the TV. Channel 57
had American Movie Classics and was playing something old
with actors he'd never seen before. He flipped to CNN, got a
round-up of world news, stared at it dully for a few minutes
with the sound dampened. Finally he scrolled till he found
local news. Controversy between city and county government,
then somebody criticizing Rio Nuevo, demanding an audit.
The governor announced a budget shortfall of millions for the
next fiscal year. Then a police report of a home invasion on
Spring Brook Drive – Zeb turned the sound up.

The four victims were all unidentified as yet, the reporter
said. There was one known survivor, also unidentified, who
had fled the rescue vehicle taking him to the hospital. A search
for him was ongoing.

One survivor. Robin? No way to know. *They sure as hell
aren't talking about me, anyway.* He hadn't been in any rescue
vehicle today.

It sounds like they don't even know I was there. The cold
knot of terror that had been coiled like a snake in his belly
since late afternoon began to dissolve. He stretched his legs,
took a long, cold drink of beer and then another. *They don't
even know I was there . . .* or was this a trap? On TV the cops
held back some details and tricked the 'perps' into making
mistakes . . . he hadn't actually perpetrated anything but some
glass-cutting, but when four people died . . . *I gotta stay out
of sight for a while. Till I see how this is going . . . Jeez, it
looks like I might be OK, though.* He stretched. *Couple more
minutes and I'll clean up the kitchen.*

Janet found him there, asleep in front of the six a.m. news, with the sound off. Alarmed by the jumping light when she walked in, she stood in the open doorway with the key in her hand, hardly breathing. She ventured one cautious step into the room, her gaze held by the glowing images of fresh morning faces on the screen. Two steps later she saw her brother slumped in the facing chair, an empty beer can at his elbow.

She sniffed the air and charged into the kitchen. The top of the stove was spattered with grease; the dirty pan and plate were in the sink. She had exactly an hour and a half to shower, get dressed, have breakfast and get to work. Driving home from the one-night stand she already regretted, she had planned it all down to the last move.

One great cry of rage came out of her as she crossed the room and grabbed him by his tousled Justin Bieber 'do, which seemed custom-cut for a sister to get a good grip. Once she had him in hand she punished him in a silence punctuated only by gasps and grunts, dragging him across the foyer and flinging him out the door.

Zeb was still half asleep and too confused to fight back. The shock and pain fit right in with yesterday, so for a few seconds he assumed the police had found him after all and must have decided to give him what he sort of, in a way, had coming. By the time he came fully awake he was on the stoop in front of Janet's door, clutching the scalp she had just released, wondering how much hair she had managed to pull out. Were there clumps of hair on the floor? Was he partly bald now?

When he found his voice he pleaded with her to let him back in long enough to get his bedroll. Pointing one accusing finger liked a poison dart, she hissed, 'Don't you move from that spot!' and flounced away. She was back in a few seconds dragging the shabby open bag with his extra underwear and shirt spilling out. She flung it at his feet and told him, in a voice shaky with rage, 'If I ever find you here again I'll call the police.'

Zeb cried out, 'Wait, my dark glasses!' just as the door slammed. He heard the deadbolt lock slide to and knew she was not going to open it again – the glasses were gone.

He was on his knees, rolling up the bag, when a rumpled

man in a bathrobe came out of the next apartment demanding to be told what in hell was going on out here. Zeb told him to go shit in his hat, starting another loud argument that soon brought several more neighbors out of surrounding apartments. He left them all there yelling at each other in the sunshine of a perfect May morning and walked toward the bus stop with his bedroll on his back.

Halfway there he remembered he didn't have enough change left to get on board a bus. Unable to think of another destination – he knew no one on this street but his sister – he kept on walking toward the bench and sign.

There were several buses on this route that would take him downtown. That's where he would have to go, he decided, for whatever he decided to do next – beg, borrow or steal, what else was there?

When he got to the stop he counted the change he had left – fifty-five cents. There was nobody on the bench but a drably-dressed old woman with bad hair clutching a scuffed leather purse. She was arranging canvas bags around her on the seat, and talking to herself. Or to the bags? Either way he was having nothing to do with her. But with the optimism of the habitual sponger, he told himself that by the time his bus came he would surely find one person understanding enough to give him seventy cents.

NINE

Will stood by the bed, looking tentative, holding a cup of coffee. 'Your note said to wake you at eleven,' he said.

'Mmf.' She surfaced from deep REM sleep. Her brain trailed wisps of a menacing dream, hostile creatures stalking her through a featureless desert . . . Still fighting them off with part of her mind, she sat up slowly, pulling pillows behind her, and squinted at Will through sticky eyes. He set the coffee down and turned the handle toward her. Carefully, feeling unsteady, she picked it up and took a sip. Hot. Good, though, going down. Maybe tomorrow she could get up. 'Thanks.'

He pushed her knees over and nested in the curve. 'What time did you get to bed?'

'Little after three.' She drank some more coffee, said, 'Aaahh,' and squeezed his hips with her legs. 'This is good. What about you, did you sleep at all?'

'Couple of hours. Took Aggie to her appointment at ten.' The cruelest after-effect of Aggie's stroke was that her peripheral vision was damaged so she couldn't drive. Convinced her eyes would heal soon she had not surrendered her driver's license or sold her car. Sarah dreaded the day she had to give it up.

'Thanks for doing that. Everything go OK?'

'Doc said she's doing fine, just needs to watch the blood pressure. On the way home she said, "I already gave up butter and salt and eggs, I'm running out of things to give up." I wanted to mention bacon, but she's a little grumpy today.'

'She knows she shouldn't eat bacon. But all those years on the ranch . . . my Dad liked bacon and eggs for breakfast, so that's what she cooked. "Forty years of teaching my body to need bacon," she calls it.' She touched his arm, felt a surge of lust. *Damn, there's never enough time.* 'You'll get some more rest this afternoon, right?'

'You bet. And you'll get home on time tonight, we all hope. Aggie said, "Tell her I'm making meat loaf and baked potatoes – that'll get her home."'

'Ah, she knows me well.'

'Good. And tomorrow morning early, when I get home from work?' His scanty gray eyebrows did the best imitation they could manage of Tom Selleck in his *Magnum P.I.* days. 'I'm gonna collect on those. Thanks for the snack.'

She giggled, said, 'Deal,' finished her coffee, threw off the covers and sniffed. 'Right now, though, don't get downwind of me till I've had a shower. Hoo! What a night!'

Will called after her as she headed for the bathroom, 'Two poached eggs? How soon?'

'Twenty minutes. Whole wheat toast if we've got it. Thanks.' Turning and soaping under the pounding water, feeling the fatigue and anxiety of the long night's work sluice away, she asked herself, *How did I ever get along without that man?*

Toweling off, she thought about work. Delaney had sent them all home from the crime scene, staying on himself to see to the late deposit of the money. There'd be a lot more talk about that today. There was an ongoing Attempt to Locate notice being passed from shift to shift, so every patrolman in town was searching for the ex-dead-guy. His existence had been kept from the media. Will hadn't mentioned him just now, so she knew there'd been no arrest by the time he left work at six. Maybe the radio . . . Oh, well, she'd know soon enough. Better get dressed fast now.

Soon as you can make it after lunch, Delaney had said about today's work schedule. Maybe he should have said, '*If* you can make it,' she thought, watching four detectives straggle into their work stations a few minutes after one. They were all showing the aftermath of exhaustion, an ache like no other. Sarah felt as if her depth perception was a little off, and sounds were strangely muted. They were all moving carefully, as if afraid of falling, and Delaney's voice had a dry rasp.

They knew there was only one cure for what ailed them – tired or not, get to work, find some answers to the many questions left hanging when they boarded up the house. But there was a lot of inertia. They all sat in their cubicles doing busy work, answering emails and returning phone messages, till Delaney got his desk clear and called them all into his office, saying, 'Come on, we've got to prioritize.'

'That part of my brain is still asleep,' Jason said. 'I could probably do some prioritizing for you by tomorrow afternoon.'

Delaney shook his head. 'Everybody, call your snitches,' he said. 'See what's out there about the Klutzbach brothers. Who was with them when they tried to invade that house?'

'OK,' Ollie said, 'but first I have to check all the weapons and ammo into evidence. I secured it last night in one big box and told the evidence tech not to touch it till I get back in here today.'

'Fine,' Delaney said, 'do that right away. Oh, and while you're at it, make me that list of guns you talked about, with all the spent ammo you found and what's left in each weapon.'

'I said that? Damn, what a memory,' Ollie said. His jokey daytime persona was coming back. When Delaney frowned, he said, 'OK, you got it.'

'I'd like to find some of those neighbors at work,' Ray Menendez said. 'I got a few phone numbers last night and maybe with a city directory . . . if I could catch them in the daytime when their kids aren't around . . .'

'Try it,' Delaney said. 'We sure didn't get much so far. But go after your snitches too – you always seem to have some good ones.'

'Yeah,' Ray said, smiling fondly, 'I know the baddest guys.'

'And Jason? I want you to get in touch with the Tucson narc squad, the guys who picked up the weed. I'll give you the names and numbers. See if they can tell us any more about this shipment now that they've had a look at it. Or if they've got any leads on the two men in the house.'

'I can do that,' Jason said happily. He loved schmoozing with guys from the narc squad. They made big busts, got their pictures in the paper. Not as well funded and glamorous as DEA guys, but he would trade for one of their jobs in a heartbeat. Kept you away from domestics – idiot couples beating on each other.

'Oscar, you find the carpet cleaner?'

'Yes. He's coming into town today. Soon as I call him he'll come and see me.'

'Call him now, get him in here. He might have a hunch who took his van; sometimes they see somebody stalking and don't think about it till later. And Sarah, you . . .'

'I keep thinking about Josephina, the woman with the babies who called in the shooting. Can you give me some time at her house? Maybe have Ray go along and introduce me? All due respect, but I was thinking, maybe with another woman . . .' Delaney was nodding, thinking about it, but as usual their conversation was interrupted by a phone call. He looked at the caller ID, said, 'Wait,' to Sarah, and into the phone, 'Yes, Doctor?'

There was a burst from a loud voice and Delaney said, 'She's right here.' He handed the phone to Sarah, saying, 'Greenberg.'

'Been a silly kerfuffle down here,' the doctor said, yelling over some background noise. 'I end up with time to autopsy one of your shooters this afternoon. Make any difference to you which one I do?'

'Um . . . yes. Let's do Mr Brush Cut.'

'Mr who?'

'Sorry.' Having worked all night with the monikers they'd assigned to their many John Does, she'd forgotten they were not proper names. 'The black-haired man from inside the house.'

'OK. Why no hesitation? Something special about this guy?'

'We think he was the last man standing. We've got four weapons, and we'd like to know which one killed him.'

'Great Scott – a mystery. OK, get down here fast and we'll see what we can find.'

She handed back the phone.

'What is it?' Delaney said. 'You look surprised.'

'Moon must be blue. Greenberg's cheerful.'

He still looked pretty amiable an hour later when Sarah faced him in the operating room at the ME's office on District Street. They both wore slippery plastic gowns, caps and booties the color of a swamp. Their voices were pitched a little louder than usual, in an effort to combat the tinny echo off scrubbed metal surfaces. Between them lay the naked body of a well-muscled, thirty-something man who, except for being dead on a cold steel table, appeared to be in great shape.

Greenberg's movements were supple and sure as he prepared the body for surgery. He was in his element here, his usual Type-A pickiness ameliorated. Recording his findings as he worked, he looked reasonable and confident. And who but Greenberg, she reflected, would have thought to ask her which body she'd like to examine first?

The shot that had creased the victim's scalp was of no significance, he said. But he had found the fatal gunshot wound, no bigger than a dime, under the victim's abundant dark hair.

'We can only see one entry wound on this body,' the doctor said, speaking into his recorder before the cutting began, 'on the back of the neck, just above the hairline. There is no evidence of an exit. There is a burn ring around the wound, indicating a very close-range shot . . .'

He made the great Y cut that opened the body and began removing remarkably sound organs, one after another. Their basic good health contrasted powerfully with the disastrously opened corpse and the rigid set of the dead face. 'Look at this,' he said, cradling the dead man's liver tenderly in his gloved hands, 'we should all have a liver like this one.'

Finally he made the cut across the top of the brush cut, peeled the scalp down over the face, sawed a quarter-moon slice out of the skull and lifted out the drastically damaged brain. The bullet had pierced the brain stem and plowed through the right hemisphere, caromed off the heavy plate of bone above the eyebrows and criss-crossed to the skull behind the left ear before burying itself in the midbrain.

'Of course, we can't really see the fatal kink that was the real cause of his death,' he said after tracing the wound track. 'It's too bad stupid ideas don't leave a scar, isn't it? Maybe we could find a cure for the next generation of crazies.' He laid what was left of the brain gently in the weighing dish and finished his riff. 'If this fool hadn't become convinced that drug-dealing and murder were sensible ways to earn a living, you can see by these flawless innards, Sarah, that he could have had a long, comfortable life.'

He was always so respectful of the bodies, Sarah thought. Death absolved them, somehow, in his eyes, of the inane futility he saw in his fellow humans while they lived.

The single bullet had bounced around through brain tissue, reducing much of the beautifully subtle organization to a bloody pulp. 'All in a few seconds,' Greenberg said, 'and even so he was probably dead before the destruction was finished. Soon as a high-velocity slug like this one' – he tweezed it out and laid it gently on a soft napkin – 'goes through a brain stem, as it did right here, it's over in a blink.'

'This autopsy introduced a very interesting twist,' Sarah told her fellow detectives at the end of the day. They were all gathered in Delaney's office again when she got back to the station. 'The shot that killed Brush Cut could not have come from outside the house.'

'So somebody did get in through the window,' Ollie said, 'and shot him from behind?'

'From right up close behind,' Delaney said. 'Is that what you're saying?'

'A contact shot. Yes.'

Ollie said, 'You think it was the tricky ex-dead-guy that got away?'

'Unless it was the guy with the wonderful tats in Barney's photo,' Ray said. 'Wouldn't the chief be happy if we nailed him with the photo equipment he fought so hard to get in the cars?'

'What if it was his own partner?' Jason said. 'Mr Desert Eagle.'

Ollie said, 'That's not possible, is it?'

'I don't think so,' Sarah said. 'Pretty sure that was a .22 slug I just turned in.'

'No use speculating till the crime lab processes the slug,' Delaney said. 'They'll tell us if it matches any of the four weapons we've collected here.'

'If it does,' Ollie said, 'we have to figure out how that could possibly work with the crime scene as we've sketched it.'

'Which is going to take some very fancy figuring if you ask me,' Ray said.

'But maybe no fancier,' Delaney said, 'than explaining how anybody but a lunatic would climb in that window with bullets flying all around and run up close enough to a guy firing an AK47 to shoot him in the back of the head.'

'Yes – unless he has very long arms, he had to get really close. Think about that,' Sarah said. 'And if I'm right about what went on here, that's not the most amazing thing he did.'

'Aw, come on – what else?'

'He must have thought he had some time, probably. Wouldn't you, if you'd just shot the last man standing? We're spread pretty thin in Tucson right now. Sometimes a first response can seem to take forever. But Barry was only a couple of blocks away when he got the call, he said. He hit the siren and got here while the yard was still full of smoke.'

'So . . . almost as soon as he'd killed the last man standing,' Oscar said, 'it was too late to run away.'

'Exactly. This is the part that kind of spooks me, because it means we're dealing with a guy who just doesn't give up. If I'm right, when this home invader heard the sirens, he must have tucked that small, lethal weapon back in his underpants—'

'Hides it behind his junk where you can't find it on a pat-down,' Jason said. 'Practical man.'

'Yes, and then crawled under the corpse of the man he'd just killed and played dead till he decided it was time to pretend to wake up and get us to haul him out of here.'

Jason nudged Oscar's elbow and said, 'Get this woman wound up, she sounds just like Inspector Poirot, don't she?'

'If all that's true,' Ray said, 'and I gotta say, it sounds way over the top . . . but are you thinking he expected to have time to find the money?'

'He must have had a pretty good idea where it was,' Sarah said. 'Why else would he break in? But the part that's driving me a little nuts is . . . think how fast his reaction times have to be. If he thought he could get the money and get away in that cleaning van . . . and then Barry's siren started, almost as soon as the shooting stopped. Most guys would just give up and run then. But he stayed, for the two or three minutes it took Barry to get here. And *then* had the presence of mind to crawl under the man he'd just killed.' She looked around at the tired crew wanting to go home. 'He thinks on his feet just fine. So what was he doing there all that time?'

'You can't expect to answer all the questions with one bullet,' Delaney said. 'Quit trying to solve the case before all the information's in. I want you all to go home on time and get a good night's sleep.'

'Aw, don't be such a weenie,' Ollie said. 'We were all counting on working all night.'

'I bet. Tomorrow Sarah's got to watch all the other autopsies, and the rest of you have got to follow up on phone calls and interviews. Jason, you still have to sketch the scene, right? You're all recording everything you find? Keeping careful notes?'

'I haven't had time to type up my notes,' Sarah said, 'and I won't tomorrow.'

'Put it all on your desk and put a brick on it. The chief loves how much money we found, by the way. He's already planning the awards and the photos.'

'Ooh, photos, where'd I leave my blusher?' Jason said.

Back at their desks, they checked their emails and closed their PCs. 'Hey, I love driving home in daylight,' Ray said. 'Maybe I'll barbeque tonight.' He called home to ask his partner if she'd started anything. Everybody in the section started salivating as Ray and his girlfriend debated the relative merits of brats and ribs.

'Exhausted again!' Jason said, slumping against his car in the parking lot. 'Must be quitting time.'

'And, hey, the good news is we got the money, so the chief is happy.' Ollie said. 'Isn't the drug business wonderful? It works for everybody!'

TEN

A van with Hannah's Housemaids painted on the side pulled in at the bus stop and dropped off a night-shift cleaning crew from the stores in the area, four women in aprons with tired brown faces. They stood in a row, staring at Zeb like suffering saints until he got up off the middle of the one long bench. '*Gracias!*' they cried, and crowded their hard-worked haunches onto the metal seat, chattering like happy sparrows. The old lady and her packages were scrunched into a tight corner at the end.

Standing a foot away from the housemaids, Zeb watched them covertly, thinking that he must look the way he felt – like a homeless man with no money. These women had had their share of hard times, too – you could see that in their faces. Was bad luck supposed to make people more sympathetic, or less? He couldn't remember what he'd heard about that.

When they momentarily ran out of things to say and settled into patient silence, he leaned across the front of their chastely-covered bosoms and said, 'I just got beat up and robbed.'

Four broad faces turned up and watched him out of black expressionless eyes. Zeb said, 'Could one of you ladies spare me a dollar so I could get on this bus?'

They all looked at each other. Turning back to him, the oldest one said, '*No hablo Inglés.*'

Zeb moved a couple of steps farther away and studied his shoes.

As a bus marked Downtown approached, a thin gray-haired man trotted across the parking lot from the Valencia Apartments, reaching the bench just as the bus pulled in. As the doors hissed open, Zeb stepped up to the lightly panting man, told him he had just lost his wallet, and asked for three quarters. The gray-haired man snarled, 'Get away from me, you freak,' and climbed aboard.

The cleaning crew climbed aboard behind him and sat

together in the back. The bus belched carbon residue at the
bench and rolled away. Zeb sat down again by the old woman
and stared dully across the street as the sun rose higher and
the street grew busier.

Two more people came down the long slope from some
houses behind the apartment complex, housewifey women
with large purses, chatting as they walked. They looked solid
and certainly solvent, but not sympathetic. Just in case, though,
Zeb rehearsed new lines in his head. When they came to the
bus stop and sat down, he told them right away how he had
just awakened after a night in the bars, found that his wallet
had been stolen, and now in order to get to the bank and start
repairing his life he had to solve this problem: how to get on
this bus with only fifty-five cents?

'What a tough break,' one of the ladies said. 'Where do
you live, honey?'

'Well . . .'

'That's what I thought.' She pulled a small digital camera
out of her purse and snapped his picture. 'My husband is a
security guard at St Mary's and he has access to police records.
Look at this worthless scum,' she told her friend, 'with his
eyebrow ring and that shit on his arms. He'll be easy to identify. So the next time either one of us sees you in this
neighborhood,' she said, turning on Zeb angrily, 'we'll have
you arrested, Deadbeat.' A bus pulled in just then. As she
climbed aboard, she said loudly to her friend and everybody
else on the bus: 'We've had enough of these homeless loafers
around here; we're not putting up with them any longer.'

Zeb got ready to flip her the bird but she never looked back.
He stood in his dorky T-shirt, very rumpled, squinting into the
punishing morning glare, wishing he had his sunglasses.
Yesterday morning at about this time, he reflected, he had
been wearing a sporty cotton-and-spandex shirt with many
secret pockets that he'd intended to stuff full of stolen cash.
He had escaped from that adventure without a scratch, almost
as if he lived a charmed life. But today he was being treated
like a snake because he'd asked for seventy cents. If there was
a lesson to be learned from the last twenty-four hours it was
going way over his head.

He sat down by the bag lady and stared across the street some more.

'I'll give you two dollars,' a scratchy contralto voice said, 'if you'll help me get these bags up to my house.'

Zeb looked around. The old lady with the bags was the only person here; it must have been her voice. He would not have expected it to be so strong. She was watching him through thick glasses. A floppy straw hat hid the whole top of her head. All he could see was a small mouth and pointed chin. She looked harmless, but so did his mother, who could reduce him to stammering shame with a raised eyebrow. This woman looked much older than his mother and had wild hair and a weird hat – he didn't want to deal with her at all. But she had said the magic words: two dollars.

He said, 'Where's your house?'

'See those big buildings back there?' She pointed back toward the apartment block where Zeb had spent the night. 'My house is a couple of blocks behind them.'

'Two bucks to carry bags all that way? Not a great rate of pay.'

'Well, you're not having a lot of success panhandling, are you, dear? Maybe you should take a shot at honest labor.'

He opened his mouth to tell her that usually the people who praised honest labor most were the ones who never had to do any. But he was completely out of money and getting hungry again, and she was right about his poor track record as a beggar. So he said, 'How about five?'

'Two and a half and a ham sandwich.'

For the hell of it he said, 'Three and you put a slice of cheese on it.'

'Done.' She got up and pointed to the two canvas tote bags. 'Take these.'

'Whoa,' he said, when he picked them up. 'What's in here, rocks?'

'Groceries. Including the ham and the cheese. Can you walk?'

'Of course I can walk,' he said. It wasn't easy, though. He had his bedroll on his back, too – ordinarily no great burden, but together with the bags . . . he put the bags down while she gathered her things.

When she had her purse settled on her left shoulder she picked up the third bag, a small string satchel with a few items in it. Turning toward the apartment building she said, 'What's your name?'

'Uh . . . Zeb.'

'You don't seem very certain. Do you want me to call you something else?'

'No. Zeb'll work.' He winked. 'Since that's my name.' There was no way she could know his full name was Zebulon, although what else could it be?

'OK, Zeb. You can call me Doris, for the same reason. We're going right up this street here.' She pointed east on Camino de la Tierra.

Doris was small but spry, leading the way. The sun rose higher and the morning heated up. Climbing the shallow slope, Zeb got hot and then hotter. In a few minutes his soaked T-shirt was plastered to his rib cage. Sweat trickled into his ears and down the insides of his legs.

Surely this old white-haired woman needed a rest. Any minute now she would say so. But for what seemed like a long time she didn't stop or even slow down. Finally he gasped, 'Need a breather!'

He put the bags down and leaned against a light pole. His new employer – not much of a boss, but she was certainly not a friend – watched him critically.

'You're kind of a weenie under those silly tattoos, aren't you, dear? You must be Zeb the Couch Potato, is that it?'

'Hey, these bags are heavy.' He touched one with his foot. 'How'd you expect to get them home if I hadn't come along?'

'Well, Valerie was supposed to pick me up.' She wasn't looking at him any more. 'But she was late, or maybe she forgot. Reliability isn't her strong point.'

'Oh? What is?' Zeb didn't care but he wanted to keep her talking so he could lean on the pole a little longer.

'Oh . . . she's good at climbing ladders, she's not afraid of heights. And she reads well, when she can calm down enough to sit still.'

Showing her age now, Zeb thought – talking crazy. Climbing ladders and reading? Go figure. He had heard about older people getting this Alzheimer's disease. Hadn't seen it before – his mother made unreasonable demands, but she wasn't crazy. She knew exactly what she was doing – busting balls. This woman sounded more like she was drifting through time. One minute Valerie sounded like a child, unable to sit still, but then what would she be doing up on a ladder? Or driving a car?

He was uneasy around people he didn't understand, so he picked up the bags and said, 'Ready?' as if Doris had been the one who asked for a rest.

They had already passed the side of the big apartment block where he'd spent last night. His sister would be at work now, so he was not concerned about her – she lived over on the other side, anyway.

He'd never walked along this street before, or wondered what was back here. There were clusters of small, single-family houses behind walls, then random mixes of mobile home parks and ill-kept duplexes. It was a street without a plan, he thought, and still slanting gradually upward. His arms were definitely going to fall off.

The old woman pointed to a gated driveway in the next block and said, 'My house is in there.'

Zeb said, 'Nice driveway. Let's stand here and admire it a while.' There was nothing much to look at really, a glassed-in booth in the middle of a driveway, gates that were open now but could be swung shut. This dowdy little woman didn't look well off enough to live in a gated community. Could she be a servant? She looked too old for that.

Not that he gave a damn why she was here if she'd feed him and pay him. Zeb worried that she intended to get her bags home and then try to stiff him. How much of a hurt would he have to put on her to get her to pay up? He couldn't quite see himself eating a sandwich in front of a whimpering old dame he'd just raised a lump on.

Then again this whole scenario seemed so unlikely, walking bags of rocks 'n' groceries up an endless hill with Evil Granny Doris – off and on he considered that maybe heat and stress had done a number on his brain and he was making it all up. But Evil Granny kept bringing him back to earth with little verbal jabs, asking if he was going to faint and like that. She knew perfectly well how heavy these bags were – she'd been sitting at the bus stop because she couldn't carry them herself. Now that she'd made him her slave, though, she was enjoying herself, mocking his pain. His sense of grievance, never far from the surface, came back big time. This had better be one hell of a ham and cheese sandwich he was sure as shit going to get. If, that is, he didn't die of exhaustion before he made it to that stupid gate that was, *fuck!*, still a block away.

By the time they turned in at the driveway he was wondering if doctors amputated dead hands or just let them hang there. He wanted to ask why there was no attendant in the booth but decided to save his breath. Doris led him along a curved street, around another curve and into a cul-de-sac.

The houses were all double-and-triple-wide manufactured homes – neat plastic houses permanently installed in small yards with flowers. Doris marched up a sidewalk between a pale pink double-wide with white trim and a carport where a car crouched under a fitted cover. She climbed two steps, unlocked a white door and said, 'Come in.'

The front of the house was a carpeted living room that continued down one side to a dining-room table with a light over it. There was a counter on the other side of a divider with a kitchen behind it, a butcher-block island with stools on one side.

'Whaddya know, we made it,' the lady said. She swung her string bag up onto the butcher block and turned on an overhead light. 'Put everything up here and sit on that stool. I'll put these things away and— My goodness, you look tuckered. You need some water?' She fetched him a glass with ice. 'Soon as I get these groceries stowed I'll make us something to eat.' She started slamming doors and humming. Rest seemed to be the farthest thing from her mind. How had she stayed so strong – was she a witch? Zeb had to hold onto his arms to keep them from shaking.

When he could let go, he drank some water and then some more. By the time the glass was empty he was strong enough to get up and pour a refill from the pitcher she'd left on the counter. When he was near the bottom of the second glass she put a plate in front of him with a big ham sandwich on dark rye, with potato salad and a dill pickle. Zeb took a bite out of the pickle and felt his taste buds wake up and sing.

They were almost finished with lunch when the front door flew open without warning. A young female with a yard of brown hair, three nose rings and very short denim pants stood in the open doorway, squinting into the room, and yelled, 'Gram?'

'We're right here, dear,' the old lady said. 'No need to yell.'

The girl slammed the door and stomped over to where they sat, talking fast. 'Where in hell have you been? You had me worried sick! I waited and waited at that filthy bus stop. Stinking diesel, Omigod, I think my lungs are destroyed.'

'What a shame,' Doris said. 'I guess that makes us even – I waited a long time for you, too.'

'Gram, we said eight o'clock, don't you remember?'

'No, Valerie, we said seven. You told me you had an early class so you couldn't give me a ride home today, so I said I'd shop early and you could pick me up at seven. This is Zeb, he helped me get home.' She nodded toward him, waved a hand toward the noisy, almost-pretty girl, and said, 'My granddaughter, Valerie Duncan.'

Zeb said, 'Hi.'

Valerie looked him over and turned back to her grandmother with a snarky little smile. 'Now, where'd you pick up Zeb, Gram?' She had switched, all of a sudden, to a jolly, teasing tone. 'Tell the truth – you been hanging out in the bars again?'

'No, dear, that's your thing to do. Are you hungry? Do you want a ham sandwich?'

'At nine o'clock in the morning? I don't think so.'

'It's ten-thirty, Valerie.'

'Whatever. You got any granola?'

'Sure. On the usual shelf, help yourself. Here's a bowl.' Valerie rummaged in a cupboard and filled the bowl, spilling some on the floor. She left it there, came back with her full bowl and parked herself on a stool by Zeb, still without speaking to him. Then she seemed to detach from her surroundings temporarily, staring around the room, itching her arms and sniffing, until Doris handed her a spoon and a carton of milk.

Her hands shook when she poured the milk, Zeb noticed. The seam was coming out of one side of her shorts, on the hip nearest him, and the underpants that showed through the tear didn't look very clean. Valerie didn't appear to be in much better shape than he was, digging into her cereal like a starved puppy. Was it possible her last twenty-four hours had been something like his? She ate fast, with little slurping noises and a lot of crunch. Like a child, he thought, but just then she raised her head, her gaze crossed his face like a scythe and she said, 'So, Zeb, you live around here?'

'Not exactly.'

'I see.' She wiped milk off her lips with the back of her hand, sat back on her stool and sniffed a couple of times, looking at him like he was the morning news and she only had time for the headlines. 'You don't exactly live around here but you drop by the bus stop from time to time to see if any older ladies need some groceries carried home, is that it?'

'Which they always do if their granddaughters spaced out the time.' He picked a paper napkin off a pile in the middle of the table and handed it to her. 'Here, have a napkin.'

'Ah, you lend a hand to younger women too, isn't that special?' She snatched it so fast, she had it in her lap before he realized he had a scratch on the back of his hand. 'Kind of like Robin Hood with tattoos.'

'Valerie,' Doris said suddenly, pulling her head out of a cupboard where she had been rearranging groceries, 'shouldn't you be in school? What happened to your early class?'

'Oh . . . it got cancelled. But I do have a lab pretty soon, I better go. Dang, I forgot my wallet in my room, Gram, could you . . .?'

'Sorry, sweetie, I spent my last bit of cash in the grocery store. You can use your campus card for lunch, though, can't you?'

'It's in my wallet. Isn't life a bitch? So can I take this apple? Thanks.' She planted a kiss in the air three inches from her grandmother's cheek and flew out the door.

Zeb heard a car start and roll away from the house.

He sat quiet a minute, waiting for the dust to settle behind this strange person, who seemed balanced somewhere between middle-class respectability and chemically-induced sleaze. Not that he gave a damn about her, but his attention had been caught by the fact that when she asked for money, her grandmother claimed to have none in the house. Doris had come through with the sandwich and then some, but was she going to try to weasel out of the three dollars she owed him? He watched her covertly, thinking a little arm-twist should be plenty to throw a scare into her. His arms still ached from those bags; he wasn't leaving without the money.

Doris was over by the door now, watching the back of Valerie's car pull away. Still with her back turned, she snatched a handful of tissue out of a box on a table, buried her face in it, and walked past him, blowing her nose. He heard her run a lot of water in the bathroom. When she came out after a few minutes, she carried three dollar bills to the island where he was sitting and laid them down in front of him on the butcher block.

'There you go. Honest pay for honest labor. How does that feel?'

'Very good!' He had hated the carrying but he did feel good about getting the money without a fight. He had been thinking there was no way you could spin beating on old ladies to make it look like great deeds. He drank the last of his third glass of water and asked, 'OK if I use your bathroom before I go?'

'Sure.' Then, as he reached for the money, she laid her hand over it and said, 'But how would you like to make these turn into a ten?'

ELEVEN

Doris unlocked the door for Zeb, showed him where the ladder hung, and helped him bring it in from the shed. Her idea of help was telling him how to make every move – don't scrape any paint off the doorway, be careful of that lamp, make sure the legs are set level. If he ever got the ladder set up to her satisfaction he was supposed to change the bulbs in the living-room ceiling fixture, the first of the two odd jobs he'd agreed to.

He'd asked her, 'How odd?'

'That's just an expression.' She made a little shushing gesture with one hand. 'All the jobs in this house are small and easy. Don't worry, you won't get a hernia.' Zeb thought she enjoyed the haggling as much as she liked getting the work done, maybe more. She was good at it, too; whenever he balked or stalled she uncorked one of those dirty digs that challenged his manhood, so he'd quit talking and just do the damn job.

The little screws that held the ceiling fixture in place gave him trouble, so his arms hurt again by the time he handed the glass globe down to her. There were three bulbs in the fixture, hung sideways against a metal plate. When she turned the wall switch, one came on. She started to debate with herself about the relative merits of getting her money's worth out of the third bulb versus changing them all at once so she wouldn't have to pay anybody to do this again for a while. When she started around the options for the second time, Zeb said, 'And if I pass out from the heat up here and fall on you, then you won't need any more light bulbs ever in the history of the damn world – won't that be a saving?'

'Mercy,' Doris said. 'You certainly can get snappish about doing a little work.' But she went and got three light bulbs and handed them up. She was like his mother after all, he decided. Bully you till you rebelled, then act all soft and hurt so you could never win. He remembered his father saying, the day he walked out, 'Women are never satisfied.'

'How would you know?' his mother yelled after him. 'You never tried to satisfy anybody but yourself.' Said it to his back as he was leaving, never even got up to watch him go.

'Maybe you better have a little snack before you tackle the next job,' Doris said as he hung up the ladder. There was that much difference from his mother, anyway – she was a feeder. 'I've got some frozen yogurt. You like raspberry swirl?'

Doris was just drinking tea, he noticed, when he was halfway through his treat. He asked her, 'What, no dessert for you?'

'I don't seem to have much of a sweet tooth any more.'

'How come you keep it around then?'

She shrugged and said, 'Valerie likes it.'

She likes the white powder more though, doesn't she? He didn't say it out loud, wasn't going to do anything to put his ten dollars at risk. He already thought of the money as his; hadn't seen it yet but was somehow sure she would come up with it. It was a stupid piddling amount, but at least he'd be able to walk out on the street again, take a bus, see some people. Not Robin, he didn't need any more of *those* capers – but somebody who'd help him get his life started again. He just had to do one more chore for this prickly old lady, so she'd give him his money and he could boogie on.

She rinsed his bowl in the sink before she led him out to the shed again, where she lifted a tarp off a pile of stuff in a corner and showed him a wheel with a flat tire.

'There's a station across the street from the bus stop,' she said.

'The bus stop where I found you? Way down there?'

'I thought I found you but yes, way down there two whole blocks. Are you listening? Go across the street and a block to the right—'

'Oh, man, it's gonna be hard to roll a tire across that big, busy street.'

'That's why God made stop lights. A block to the right there's a gas station, Eddy's Conoco. Roll it in there and they'll fix it for you.'

'You mean for you. You gonna give me the money to pay for it?'

'They'll put it on my tab.'

'Come on. Gas stations don't run tabs.'

'Eddy does, for me. I phoned him.' She looked at her watch. 'If you'll quit arguing and go now you can be back by four and I'll make you some lemonade.'

The wheel almost got away from him once on the sloping sidewalk, but he knocked it down before it ran into the street. After that he knew to stay alongside it, not behind, so he made the bus stop OK. Getting across Valencia before the light changed was a real sweat, though, so he was fagged by the time he got to the station. But then, nice surprise, Eddy was friendly.

'Helping out Doris, huh?' he said. 'Good for you. She's a nice lady.'

You should try climbing a ladder for her sometime, Zeb thought. But he didn't say it; his ten dollars was getting closer every minute so he just smiled and Eddy showed him where the water fountain was on the side of the building.

Going back up the slope with a fully-inflated tire was much harder; the damn thing seemed to have gained a hundred pounds. Who knew air weighed so much? Or was it gravity? He was very glad to see the gate to her compound but then had a terrible two minutes after he turned in when he couldn't remember where her house was. Nothing looked familiar and he began to imagine himself walking around for hours pushing that freaking tire. He got a glimpse of his reflection in a window and saw he looked crazy – sweat-soaked T-shirt, frightened face – what if somebody called the cops? Cops in cars might still be looking for him.

Around another curve, though, he found himself looking at Doris' house. He made a sound that was humiliatingly close to a sob and knocked on the door.

'Quarter past four,' Doris said. 'Not bad, considering.'

'Considering what?'

'How hot it is, for one thing. And the fact that you're really in rotten shape. Don't you ever get any exercise? Let's put that wheel away and get you a cold drink.'

When he'd washed his hands and sat down in front of a

tall, sweating glass of lemonade, she said, 'I made a chocolate
cake yesterday. Would you like a piece?' When he said yes
she pulled a flat pan out of a cupboard and cut him a big
square. Frosted.

He'd almost finished the cake and was well into his second
glass of lemonade when she laid two five dollar bills by his
glass. 'Well, I think we did pretty well today,' she said, 'all
in all.'

'You bet.' He put the money away quickly, afraid she might
pull it back and offer another job. At the same time another
part of him wanted to stay right here in this house, doing
chores for Doris for maybe a month. The two minutes when
he was lost in her driveway had shaken him back into the
nightmare of Monday.

Doris was saying, 'So, how would you like—' when there
was a squeal of brakes just outside, a car door slammed, and
the girl with all the hair, Valerie, flew in through Doris' front
door. It seemed to be her standard way to enter a room, as if
wolves were chasing her.

'Hey, Gram, how would you like—' It was comical, the
way she echoed her grandmother's words without knowing it.
Doris grinned at her and Zeb felt himself doing the same thing.

She seemed to hate that, planted herself in a square stance
and stared from one to the other, saying, 'What's so damn
funny?' Before anybody could answer she swung her too-bright
gaze onto Zeb like a searchlight and said, 'What's the story
with you, Mr Eyebrow-ring? You're right where I saw you
last. Is that all you do here, eat?'

'No, we've been working all day,' Doris said. 'Now we're
having a snack. You want some cake and lemonade?'

'Sure.' She plunked onto the farthest stool from his, staring
at him like a treed cat. Doris trotted around, tinkling ice into
a glass, slapping down a plateful of cake and coming back
with a fork that went *clink!* onto the plate. Waiting on people
made Doris happy, Zeb saw. Her face under the wild thatch
of hair smoothed out and one side of her mouth was almost
smiling.

'You started to ask me something when you came in,' she
said. 'What was it, dear?'

'Oh, I was wondering if you wanted to go see *The King's Speech*,' Valerie said. 'We talked about it, remember? But of course we didn't know then,' her voice was heavy with sarcasm, 'that this hero with all the tattoos was going to come along and turn into a house guest.'

'Well, he hasn't done that,' Doris said, 'but we are pretty busy here right now. Planning tomorrow's work,' she added, letting her eyes rest on Zeb for a few seconds. Zeb nodded and kept his mouth shut. 'So I hope you'll give me a rain check on the movie, will you?'

Zeb wasn't sure what Doris had in mind. He was going along with her, though, because she was the one with the cake and lemonade. She seemed to want to both keep this trouble-some girl nearby and fend her off. You can sure tell they're family, he thought. They've got all the tricks.

Valerie seemed to get whatever message Doris was sending. She said, 'Fine,' bolted the last piece of cake, slammed down her fork, stood up, and drank the last of her lemonade standing. Fished through a drastically overloaded backpack till she found her keys, said, 'See ya,' to her grandmother and sailed out the door without another glance at Zeb.

The silence she left behind her was like a hole in the room.

Finally Doris, with her face all puckered up again, began picking up dishes and stacking them in the dishwasher. The clock on the stove said quarter to five. Zeb walked over to his bedroll in the corner and picked it up. 'Guess I better hit the road,' he said. Halfway to the door he turned and asked her, 'Do you really have a job you want to get done tomorrow or was that just . . .'

'Oh.' Doris came back gradually out of whatever cloud she was in. 'I was wondering if you could put the wheel back on my car and help me get it started.'

'What's wrong with it? Besides the wheel.'

'Um. Might be a wire loose on the battery.'

'Well, I'm not a mechanic.'

'I don't think it's anything complicated.'

'I don't have any tools.'

'I do. Do you always stand around and argue before you start anything? No wonder you're not getting any place.'

'How do you know I'm not getting any place? You don't even know me.'

'I found you this morning begging change at a bus stop, remember? So I kind of figure you haven't made a big mark in the world yet.'

'Fine. Just forget it then.' He slung his bedroll on his back and walked to the door as he fastened the straps.

He was reaching for the door handle when she said, 'I'll pay you twenty dollars if you'll get my car started tomorrow and help me run a couple of errands.'

'Is it going to take all day? Twenty dollars isn't enough to . . .' He ran out of breath suddenly and stopped talking, wondering if he was having a heart attack. Staring at the panels in Doris' door, he realized what he wanted more than anything in the world was to spend tomorrow in the drab carport of this fading pink house, tinkering with Doris' car. It was safe here and the food was good.

To save face he asked her, 'Does this offer include lunch?'

TWELVE

'I missed out on everything that happened here yesterday,' Sarah said Wednesday morning. 'Did what's-his-face from Oracle come in to see you, Oscar?' He was sitting in his work station, pressed and perfect as always, but he was staring at his PC with what looked like growing alarm.

He turned his face a reluctant three inches toward her, still looking at the screen. 'Ed Benson,' he said. 'Yes, he did.' He detached from the screen finally, blinked a couple of times and rearranged the crease in his pants. Sarah waited. After forty-five seconds she said, 'Well, so, you took him to the impound yard?'

'Yes.' He sounded as if he had something stuck in his throat.

'Did he ID the van?'

'Yes.'

'And?'

'He gave me the customer's phone number and they verified that he was in their house, cleaning the carpet, when the van was stolen.' He cleared his throat again before he said, 'He about gagged when I told him he can't have it back right away.'

'Yes. Rules of evidence are hard on working people.' Oscar seemed to be doing some gagging himself. 'Are you sick?'

'I just realized I must have made a mistake.' His throat closed up momentarily on the word 'mistake.' He had stumbled badly on his first case after he joined the department, and ever since then he had been trying to turn in perfect days so Delaney would stop thinking about recommending he go back to auto theft. He was so conscientious and detail-oriented he made the rest of the squad look slapdash. They were all trying to help him lighten up a little.

He pointed at his screen and said, 'Look here.'

Sarah looked at the report, where an unfinished sentence read, 'Edward Benson states that he parked his van in front

of a house near the corner of North Alvernon and Seneca
Streets shortly after two p.m. By three, he was inside, cleaning
the carpet, when he heard the engine start. He ran outside . . .'

'OK, I'm looking,' Sarah said. 'Where's the mistake?'

'Barry White says he arrived at the crime scene at 4:32 p.m.
Monday afternoon,' Oscar said.

'So?'

'So the corner of North Alvernon Street and Seneca Street
is, what, about ten miles from the house on Spring Brook
Drive?'

'As the crow flies, maybe. To drive it, more like twelve. So
. . . Oh.' She watched him fidget. 'That does seem like kind
of a stretch, doesn't it?'

'To steal a carpet cleaner's van that you couldn't have known
was going to be there, drive it twelve miles in Tucson traffic,
assemble a crew and invade a stash house a little more than
an hour later? Yes, I'd say that's a stretch.'

'So call him back. You must have heard him wrong.'

'I guess I'll have to.' He kicked the leg of his desk. 'Damn!
I hate it when I do something stupid.'

'Oscar, you made a mistake and you caught it. Do you want
to go on Facebook and cry about it or do you want to finish
the report?'

'You got a mean edge to your lip sometimes, you know
that? Why don't you get out of my space and let me fix this?'

'Hey, you're welcome!' She left him furiously punching
numbers and went on toward her own workspace, stopping
wherever she found another detective. She was trying to catch
up on the skinny before the call came from the ME's office.
After that she'd be in the morgue watching autopsies for
hours.

'Then I'll be even farther behind all the rest of you,' she
told Jason. 'So tell me, did you learn anything from the narcs
yesterday?'

'They claim it's plain old Mexican weed,' Jason said. 'Just
regulation naughty stems looking for the dirty dollar. The
narcs'll burn it eventually, but it's gotta go to the end of a
long queue.' He leaned back in his chair and sighed. 'I like
the locals fine but they don't have charisma like the feds, do

they? Them DEA guys, you ever take a good look at their badges? I mean,' his voice dropped to a sibilant whisper, 'Special Agent.' He patted his glossy dome, which was shaved to chocolate perfection. 'Don't that just about curl your toes?'

'Just about. You get anything from snitches?'

'Nah. Ray did, I think. I heard him bragging about how street he is.'

'And every word of it is true.' She followed happy noises to Ray's cubicle, where he was telling tall tales to a couple of cold-case detectives.

'Yeah, I still got my connections,' Ray told her, flashing his neon smile, shooting his cuffs. 'Two years in that gang unit was the best thing ever happened to me.' He loved to play the cool hand, show he could dredge up fresh dirt from the barrios, be a player in both worlds. Besides that, these days he knew he looked good enough to lick. He had moved in with a beautiful girl who was so thrilled by the shine of her engagement ring that she was ironing his shirts to glossy perfection.

Sarah asked him, 'Aren't your connections getting a little long in the tooth for gang stuff by now?'

'Aw, you know, a lot of those guys never get over themselves. And even the ones who finally get jobs and wives and start looking after some of their kids, they still get back to the old crack house every so often, sit under the ramada and shoot the shit. It's like an early family they can't quite leave behind.'

'They reminisce about the good old knife fights?'

'Not in so many words. Just some hand signals, some eye rolls, maybe a name and a nod. It may be bad opera but it's their opera, you know?'

'So what are they singing this week?'

'Word is the Klutzbach brothers have been seen riding around with a smooth-faced wise guy named Rolly. Or maybe Richard or Robin.'

'He uses different names?'

'Sounds like he uses everything that doesn't use him first.'

'What's his game?'

'Anything that moves. He sells a little meth around town, moves a few guns across the border. But his real specialty,

my guys say, is putting a hurt on somebody and taking whatever they've got.'

'You think Rolly might be our ex-dead-guy?'

'I kind of like him for it. You know how we keep getting
amazed by how quick and resourceful he is?'

'The way he thinks on his feet and doesn't quit. Yes.'

'Well, the gang-bangers say that's a fair description of ol'
Rolly. They got downright respectful when they talked about
how fast he is with a balisong.'

'A what?'

'You know – that butterfly knife that guys flip in Asian
slasher flicks. Jaime said, "That Rolly's some heavy shit. You
go after him, don't play nice. You see him pull out the balisong,
you kill him right away." I asked him, "Why don't you guys
kill him?" and he sort of shuddered and said, "Only if I got
to." '

'Sounds like our guy.'

'Sure does.'

'They have any idea where he hangs out?'

'Jesus says he used to have a pad on MacArthur Street, near
the rodeo grounds.'

'You didn't get a number?'

'Not far from Ricky's Sports Bar is all he could remember.
Anyway, Jaime says he thinks he lives under his hat now,
moves in with chicks and like that.'

'That doesn't sound like a steady cash flow.'

'Which is a really good reason to knock over a stash house,
no?'

'Good point. Well . . . are your bad boys going to help you
find him?'

'And get a rep on the street for snitching? Not hardly. But
Jaime said behind his hand he'll call me if he sees him.'

'You think he'll do it?'

'He might. I did him a favor once.'

Sarah's phone call came through just then, so she didn't
have to hear about the favor. Doctor Bernie Olbermann said,
'Three very studly and awesomely smart physician types are
waiting for you down here at the morgue, lady.'

'Well, there you go, see, I was just born lucky,' Sarah said.

'Be right there.' She shoved a notebook and two fresh pens into her briefcase.

She was ready to go when Delaney walked out to his crew and said, 'Listen up. I've been on the phone with the lab, asking where our DNA report is. They say it's still cooking but they should have it for us before lunchtime.'

'Oh, good,' Ollie said, 'then we'll know for sure who it is we can't catch.'

'Trouble with Ollie,' Jason said, 'is he just can't seem to stifle his enthusiasm.'

She found the forensic surgeons under punishingly bright lights, already draped in plastic and taking turns at the X-ray machine – they had decided to do all three remaining autopsies at once this morning. Sarah got into the gown and booties quickly and began trotting from room to room, making notes. She spent the most time watching Homer Klutzbach's autopsy, which so enthralled Moses Greenberg that he was silent for the better part of two hours, except to describe to his recorder the body part from which he was digging still another piece of lead.

'Let's see, cause of death,' he said near the end. 'Damn good question. Maybe we'll use that thing they used to say in westerns, hmm? "He died in a hail of gunfire." ' Homer had been shot in the left ear, right cheek, right kidney, left lung, the clavicle, pancreas and spleen. 'Two through-and-through shots also, right thigh and calf – you'll have to dig them out of the yard yourselves. How in hell did he manage to run all the way to the sidewalk in this condition?'

'In some ways Homer was born to be a champ, I think,' Sarah said, looking ruefully at the scraps that were left of him. 'He just never learned to make good choices.'

'Good choices? Oh, that's priceless!' Greenberg laughed out loud, a rare sound. 'Where'd you learn that, kindergarten?'

'I suppose.'

'I bet you were a little whiz at holding hands while you crossed the street.' He was still chuckling as she left the room, muttering, 'Good choices, Jesus.'

Why is it so easy to make fun of good behavior, she wondered, even for us who spend our lives cleaning up after misbehaving wretches? In the next room, Doctor Bernie stood over the corpse of Old Baldy, aka Mr Desert Eagle.

'Looks like the two gut shots came first,' he said. 'They both hit his heart, see? That's what all this fragmented tissue is. After those two shots he was dead, of course, so the three wounds he got lying down hardly bled at all. This one plowed right through his brain and throat and lodged in his trachea. These two shoulder shots: the one on the left went through the trapezius muscle and ended up in his spine. On the right the bullet entered through the deltoid, crossed the chest cavity here and tore through the superior lobe of his right lung and plowed right along to the left anterior. All potentially fatal wounds, but they didn't bleed much because his heart had already stopped.'

'So . . . five shots. All from the Smith & Wesson? Oh well, we won't know that till the lab tells us, will we?'

'Well, not from me, anyway,' Bernie said. 'I'm a doc, not a firearms expert. All I know is the guy who fired the last three shots wasted his ammo.'

Another bad choice, Homer. You should have run away sooner.

In the third operating room, Dr Reynaldo Valdez had opened the body of Earl LeRoy Klutzbach. Valdez was the newest forensic scientist on the ME staff, midway in his first week on the job. They were trying to break him in easy, Greenberg said, so they had given him Earl's autopsy because it appeared simplest – demonstrably, the man had been shot in the face.

Earl's right eye was undamaged, though, and after Valdez looked into it and inspected what was left of Earl's complexion, the doctor put on an extra pair of gloves, told Sarah not to touch anything, and sent some blood out to be tested. By the time he'd seen the shrunken liver, the test came back positive and Valdez said, 'Earl was lucky to get off the planet with one quick blast in the face. He had hepatitis C. See here? Cirrhosis of the liver.'

'Oh? Well, he did a long stretch in prison.'

'Where they learn some very ugly habits. See how dark his urine was? Bet it already hurt to pee. You can see the jaundice in his eye, the one he's got left. The rest of this man's life was going to be very short on pleasure.'

Sarah had worn her most comfortable cross-trainers but her legs were already screaming for relief. She had always found standing in one cold spot for a long time, which you had to do to watch an autopsy, more exhausting than an all-day hike with any amount of climbing. She asked Bernie, 'How can you tolerate it every day?'

'I can't. My feet and legs are ruined, my kids call me cow-foot. I'm designing a harness so I can dangle from the ceiling while I work.'

Walking out felt like an escape. It was just past noon and Tucson was having, no surprise, a beautiful, cloudless day in the mid-nineties. Tourists and snow-birds thought this was way too hot and had already fled but Sarah, like the rest of the Tucson natives, had a different perspective. Soon it would be June, the hardest month of the year in Tucson, dry and well above a sizzling hundred degrees. *So let's enjoy what we've still got here*, she thought, and slid the window down. She left the radio off to enjoy the drive back to the station in breezy quiet.

But she couldn't stop thinking about the four dead men lying in their cold storage bins, their vital organs neatly tucked inside their shells in no useful order. It kept eating at her, so many lives lost – *for nothing but money*. What a waste! But if you think about it they're just an exaggerated version of the way we all waste our lives, she thought – always talking about money, wishing we had more. *Getting and spending, we lay waste our powers . . .*

How much money have I made in my life so far? Hundreds of thousands. It's never felt like enough, and at the end of every year it's all gone. This big, rich country – millions of us working our butts off and every day we worry: do I make enough money? Will I have enough?

Deciding how much is enough is getting trickier every day, too. The price of gas is going through the roof suddenly, and as for groceries, Aggie said yesterday, 'I never thought I'd feel guilty buying peppers.'

Yet there's always a ready market for an eight-ball of coke

at a hundred-plus dollars a pop. And last Sunday's *New York Times* was filled with advertisements for fifteen hundred dollar bags, three thousand dollar shoes. While politicians yell about debt, nothing but debt as far as the eye can see, and say they have no choice but to cut funds for children's health care, they also want to cut taxes on the top two per cent of earners. What are we building here, Versailles? Am I working for a kleptocracy?

The bright streets of the city she loved looked sordid to her suddenly. On South Stone she walked into the dark cave of the station feeling relieved, as if she'd escaped a storm. *Maybe with luck I'll find somebody in here with an interesting problem that has nothing to do with money.*

'Hey, Sarah,' Delaney said. He was typing furiously and didn't stop when she walked in. 'We got a couple of breaks today.' He glanced up, said, 'What's the matter? Oh, three autopsies in one morning. Here, sit down. Have some water.'

'Thanks. Feels like I've just run a marathon with bodies for mile markers.' She sat and began to tell him about the long trot through the autopsies. 'The brother with the Glock didn't have long to live even if he'd behaved himself. Otherwise, no surprises.'

'Good. Save all your notes though, you never know what'll surprise you later.' He glanced back at his screen.

'You want to finish that report and I bet my email box is jammed.' She got up to leave but found Oscar Cifuentes blocking the door.

'I finally caught up to Ed Benson,' he said. 'I didn't make a mistake. Three o'clock is the time he gave me and he swears it's right.'

'Well, good for you,' Sarah said. 'See? Right all along.'

'OK, but what are we supposed to think? I mean, there's no way the time can be wrong on Barry White's report – he called in for backup the minute he got there.'

'An hour doesn't sound like enough time,' Delaney said. 'But if it's what everybody says happened – put it down, Oscar, and we'll see how it works when we review the case together.'

But Ray Menendez was in the doorway now too, beaming

self-satisfaction. 'I told you what the answer is. Ol' Rolly's just as hot as my guys said he is.'

'Why are you still calling him that?' Delaney said. 'I told you about the DNA report.'

Sarah said, 'Oh, it did come back?'

'Oh, right, you weren't here. Ray, get everybody back in here, will you? I found a lot more on him since I got his name. They matched him to a file in AZAFIS,' he told Sarah while they waited. 'His name's Robin Brady. Usually.'

'Not always?'

'Just as Ray said, he likes to change names.' All the other detectives were packing into his office now, so he read his info off the screen. 'He did a short stretch five years ago in the Juvenile Detention Center for petty theft, where they all start. He was plain Robin Brady then, had a school record and a birth certificate in that name. Since then his identity has been getting more indistinct. Shortly after his eighteenth birthday he served a few months under the same name in Pima County Jail for shoplifting. But the next time he went there it was to await sentencing, and he was carrying ID that said his name was Rolly Burgess—'

Ray said, 'Yeah, it's Rolly, not Roland, isn't it?'

'That's right. He had documents, a driver's license and bank account under the name of Rolly Burgess, was arrested and charged under that name. But when his fingerprints brought up a match to his juvenile record and then two other arrest records under different names, the judge stopped the proceedings and directed his lawyer to sort out his identity. And somebody did, obviously, because he served twenty-two months at the State Prison on Wilmot under the name Robin Brady. That last arrest record indicates he was also carrying a driver's license for Richard Bacon, but he claimed he was just holding it for a friend.'

'Whose picture was on it?' Sarah asked.

'Doesn't say,' Delaney said. 'He's probably good at changing the way he looks, too. You're right, Ray, the guy's evidently a chameleon.'

'You can say that again,' Sarah said. 'Dead one minute, alive the next.'

'Just like my snitches told me,' Ray said. 'Changes identity whenever he feels like it. I'm starting to love this bozo – he's crazy like a fox!'

Ollie said, 'Anything on that .22 he's packin'?'

'No firearms mentioned in any of these records.'

'My guess,' Ray said, 'it's whatever he just stole.'

'Anyway, your snitches delivered the straight stuff this time, Ray. We owe them a big one,' Delaney said. Coming from him it was remarkable praise, Sarah knew. He always insisted they troll their snitches, 'for the news that never makes the papers.' But then he could hardly stand to listen when they brought it back. He believed in forensic evidence, stuff you could take into court, and he despised the idle gossip of crime groupies. 'They're always trying to make mopes into Hollywood stars,' he would say. 'Bring me something I can bag and tag.'

A thoughtful silence fell in Delaney's office till Ollie said, 'It's not much of a record. Considering.'

'Considering what?'

'That he's a real badass. Look what he's done just since Monday.'

'Yeah, I've been wondering that too,' Sarah said. 'Why don't we already know all about a guy with as many boss moves as this one has?'

'Fair question,' Delaney said. 'Where'd he spring from?' Anyway, now that they had a name, he said, tomorrow they'd get addresses, cell phones, maybe even a bank account. 'Every law enforcement agency in the country will help – we'll tighten the noose until we get him.'

But in the meantime, he said, the chief had decided not to wait any longer to announce the big forfeiture that the work of the TPD homicide squad had enabled. 'He's got the stuff all laid out in the meeting room – money and guns and some of the coke, and a photographer's on his way, so everybody comb your hair, we're going to go get our pictures taken, right now.'

'Oh, this ought to be rich,' Sarah muttered, walking over. 'I know what I look like: death three times over.'

'None of that, now,' Delaney said. 'I want you all with your game faces on. Try to look like the crew that just won a battle in the drug war – but there's so much more to do. You know the drill.'

'Nightly Pentagon report,' Jason said. 'Gotcha.'

TV news crews were on hand with punishing lights. The chief and Delaney took turns fielding questions. When it was over the chief shook everybody's hand and patted Delaney on the back. Walking back to their own work spaces, Oscar Cifuentes said, 'The chief is a lot more down-to-earth than his wife, isn't he?'

Delaney, his face a mask of dread and distaste, asked: 'You know his wife?' Oscar's success as a swordsman was a joke in Homicide, and had almost cost him his spot on the crew.

'Oh,' Oscar said, looking sorry he'd brought it up, 'just to say hello to.'

THIRTEEN

Zeb wasted ten minutes trying to figure out why he couldn't pull the cover off the Buick before Doris came out of the house and said, 'You have to crawl under and . . . you know.'

'What?'

'Undo the ties.'

He laid on his back and pushed under with his heels. Pebbles bit into him, and cobwebs brushed his face. The ties had some kind of metal fasteners that clipped them to each other in a mysterious way.

Doris kept saying, from somewhere near his feet, 'What's the problem? They're not complicated.'

'They are when you're upside down with crap falling in your face.' Every time he moved, dirt fell off the bottom of the car. Something had just crawled over his arm. Besides, he didn't trust the cement blocks holding up the front left corner – what if this old heap fell on him? His brain parodied his own answer from yesterday's argument about light bulbs: *Then you won't need any more money ever – won't that be a saving?*

Just before whatever was biting his ankle bored all the way in to the joint, he figured out how to squeeze the end of the clip so the jaws opened and— 'OK, I got it,' he said, and scooted around undoing ties as fast as he could so he could slide out of there while he still had some skin left.

He stood up and pulled. The cover slid off at his feet. He kicked it aside, or started to, but Doris yelled as if he'd kicked her personally. She grabbed one end and started a show-and-tell about how she wanted it folded. It took a steady stream of instructions – back up a little, keep it taut so it won't wrinkle, now put these two sides together like *this*.

'Folding lessons are fun,' he said, 'but I was counting on fixing the car some time today.'

'Me, too,' she said, 'right after we finish the folding.'

He got the jack out of the wheel well where the spare tire wasn't. 'Seems to be missing,' Doris said, looking vaguely around at the yard as if the spare might have wandered out of the car and curled up by the shed. 'Have to see about that.'

But then setting up the jack . . . he tried it from the outside, kneeling on the cement, reaching in. He couldn't tell when he had it centered under the frame. And now that he'd been under there he couldn't stop thinking that if the jack wasn't set right, this junker was going to fall on him.

So in the end he got under the car again with the saber-toothed ants and stayed there till he was sure the jack was placed just right under the spot that was marked for it.

'Um,' Doris said, when he set the crank in place on the jack, 'let's be sure the hand brake is on.'

Goddamn, she was right. He had taken one of those 'Car Repairs for Dummies,' courses in high school and he remembered that admonition now. If the brake wasn't on the car could back off the jack and . . . he got another distinct vision of his body spreadeagled under a metallic gray Buick LeSabre.

But the rest of the job went all right. His heart almost failed him when the jack lifted the car two inches above the cement blocks, but Doris showed him how to set the teeth on the jack so it wouldn't slip. Holding his breath, he pulled the cement blocks away from the car and they lifted the wheel onto the lugs together. Then Doris stood by him, handing him lug-nuts and watching to be sure he got them on straight. They argued over all but one. When he got them as tight as he could by hand she said, 'Wait,' and darted into the shed. In a minute she was back and handed him a four-way lug wrench.

'How come you've got one of these?' he said.

'Well, you see, if you take care of your things and put them back where they belong, you have them when you need them.'

'Yeah, yeah, yeah,' he said. 'Always a lecture.' But he felt good, releasing the jack. The car had not fallen on him and the tire was on good and tight. Doing his best to sound like Zebulon, your go-to guy for car repair, he said, 'Now, what's this other thing we have to fix?'

'Oh,' she said, 'that isn't going to take long.'

He lifted the hood after she showed him where the catch was.

She pointed to the battery where the wire had been pulled off one terminal and handed him a pair of pliers. With Doris watching closely and giving plenty of free advice, he loosened the bolt, twisted the wire on and tightened it back up again. 'There,' he said, 'what else?'

'Nothing,' she said. 'Let's have a cup of coffee before we go shopping.'

Inside, enjoying a piece of cake with his coffee, he decided to risk it. 'You going to tell me why you disabled your car?'

'Maybe later,' she said. 'Right now I need to make a list.' She pulled a lined tablet and pen out of a drawer and sat over it, thinking. When she stopped thinking and began to write, she bent her head till her eyes were about two inches above the paper.

She isn't driving herself to the store because her eyes have gone bad. This old lady's running out of options. Maybe that's why she hasn't asked if I've got a driver's license. But then, think about it, how often do I ask anybody if he's got a driver's license? People just take it for granted. So let's be cool about the license. You don't get stopped, you don't get asked.

When Doris finished writing she stood up and said, 'Would you like to wash your hands before we go?'

'Oh . . . sure.'

He was off the stool, headed toward the bathroom, when she said to his back, 'Your shirt got kind of dirty under the car. I put one on the bed in the spare room back there, I think it'll fit you close enough. Why don't you use it today?'

Zeb had spent the last night under a jojoba bush in an empty field behind the Circle K, and washed up in the restroom of the Waffle House where he ate breakfast. He had been vaguely aware that his clothes were very dirty, but they fit right in to the general disorder of his life so he hadn't thought about it. He had plenty of clean shirts in storage, but getting his stuff out had not been a priority since he had no place to live. Oh, and he was probably wanted by the police.

He had made his bold move to become a hoodlum and failed miserably. He had never given any thought to what it took to be a good man, but this week had shown him he didn't have the stones to be a bad one. Now if this feisty old castoff queen was being kind to him, evidently he wasn't even making the grade as Mr So-so, the dorky odd-jobs man. Shee-it.

Washed up and wearing her clean shirt, he came back from the bathroom and stood at the top of the hall, embarrassed, afraid she would smile and say some TV-granny-type thing like, 'Well, that's better!' But she just said, looking at her list: 'Ready to go?' She picked up her purse and that little string bag with a couple of books in it, walked out and got in the passenger's seat cool as you please, looking like she'd had a chauffeur all her life.

They went to Eddy's Conoco first. While Zeb gassed up the car and washed the windshield Doris went inside and talked to Eddy. They were cordial at first and then serious, and she paid with a credit card. So she had a bank account. She might not be rich but she was not the bag lady he had first taken her for.

The Valencia branch library was their next stop. Zeb waited in the car. She didn't take long but she came out with two books. So evidently she could still read, although it must be hard, holding a book two inches from her nose like that.

She directed him every inch of the way, including which lane to drive in, to a tailor's shop where she picked up a skirt. It was much too short for her – she must be getting something repaired for Valerie. Kid can't even take care of her own clothes, he thought, and then remembered hearing a neighbor say, to his mother when she was sewing buttons on his shirt, 'When's he going to grow up?'

'Groceries next, I guess,' Doris said, hanging the skirt in the back.

Zeb said, 'I was wondering . . . there's a self-storage place not too far from here . . . you think we could stop by there? I could pick up some of my stuff.'

He brought out one box – mostly clothes. 'That's all?' she said.

'Enough for now,' he said, and put it in the trunk. No use making her think he was trying to move in on her, but he was pretty sure she'd let him keep it in the shed until he found a place.

She said, 'You just moving to town?'

'Nope. Lived here all my life.' He couldn't stand to talk

about his childhood and didn't dare discuss the recent past. And she had not explained the crippled car, so there was no hurry about blurting out secrets. 'So, which grocery store?'

They made two stops because she liked the meats in one place and the produce in another. 'And since I don't have to get everything on and off a bus today,' she said, 'I might as well get plenty.'

He wondered as the carts filled up, *Is she expecting company?* Whatever the plan was she seemed to be enjoying herself.

On the way into the second grocery store he noticed a rack of newspapers and bought a copy of the *Star.* 'That's yesterday's paper,' Doris said when she looked at it.

'Close enough for catching up on things,' he said. 'Haven't seen one all week.'

'I miss it myself,' she said. 'But I cancelled my subscription after I couldn't read it any more.' She looked sad for a minute. He loaded all the groceries in the trunk for her, and ran the carts back.

At home she said, 'Oh dear, it's past lunchtime.'

'Go ahead, I'll get this in.' By the time he had it all in the house she had a big sandwich waiting and a twenty dollar bill beside his plate. Halfway through his sandwich, he put it down, took a deep breath and said, 'I've been thinking.'

'Oh?' She chewed a while, drank some milk. 'What about?'

'Well . . . you've got that spare room you're not using, and you've got chores that need doing. Couldn't we figure out a swap?'

'You mean a certain number of hours' work for room and board?' She quit chewing for a minute and considered, her head on one side. 'I don't have all that many chores, really. Just occasional odd jobs.'

'But the driving,' he said. 'And the car needs to be washed. I could vacuum it inside, get it looking really nice.'

'Well,' she said. 'You're a big eater.'

'Not really,' he said. 'Mornings, coffee and toast is plenty.'

'I don't know,' she said, 'I like things kept neat.'

'Have I been throwing things around? But, hey, you like your privacy, I understand, forget I said anything.'

'Oh, well now, don't be so hasty. Now that I think of it, there's the reading. That could add up to some hours.'

'The reading?'

'Maybe you haven't noticed I have macular degeneration. That's why I can't drive.'

'So those books you got from the library—'

'Somebody has to read to me. I've been a reader all my life, I can't just stop. Valerie used to come over almost every day for an hour or two. But lately it seems like her time is pretty much taken up with her studies.'

'Well, you're right, that's another chore. Driving and vacuuming and reading. I could read a little bit from the paper every day too, if you wanted to take it again. Does that get us anywhere close to a deal?'

'Maybe so. Let's test drive the reading, shall we? You can sit in this chair, it's got the best light.' She had a book called *Our Man in Havana*, an old book, dog-eared and smelling like decay. In the very first line he choked up on the word nigger and looked up at her in surprise.

'It's an old book and there's just the two of us here,' she said. 'Go ahead.'

Zeb thought it was damn odd reading for a lady, which is what he thought you called bookish women even if you did find them slumped at a bus stop. But OK, he went on and made the best of it, had trouble with all the names and stumbled on the word colonnade. After forty-five minutes she said, 'Let's stop now and maybe have a little more after dinner? I'll show you how to work the shower and then I think I'll take a nap.'

After she showed him the shower she turned in the bathroom door, looked at him straight and said, 'You're not thinking about beating my head in while I sleep or anything, are you? I don't have much worth stealing.'

It was a fair question and he had been wondering if she wasn't thinking about it. He put on what he hoped was his sincere look and said, 'No. You want to pat me down, make sure I'm not carrying any concealed weapons?' As soon as he said it he remembered, with horror, the Lorcin pistol in the side pocket of his cargo pants. He stared at her with his mouth open for a long moment, feeling his brain freeze. Finally, in a desperate effort to explain away his horrified reaction he crossed his hands in front of his crotch and squeaked, 'Please say you won't.'

It worked. Her delighted laughter pealed in the hall, surprisingly youthful. She gave a little dismissive wave as she turned away, saying, 'Don't worry, Zeb, I'm quite sure I can resist your manly charms. Just barely, of course, but I can.' She laughed again as she turned into her own room and closed the door.

OK, so he was insulted again, but he was in – she thought he was funny, not scary. Now he'd better figure out where to stash the weapon.

He walked back into his small bedroom, looking for a hiding place. The ceiling was solid. There was a tiny closet with nothing hanging in it yet. He didn't have enough clothes to put in the dresser drawers to hide anything under. The bed . . . she might take a notion to change his bed without telling him, but . . . there was a box spring and a mattress. She was small, with short arms. He shoved the Lorcin all the way to the center, between the spring and mattress, backed out and smoothed the covers.

The home invasion on Spring Brook Drive was one of the lead stories in Wednesday's paper. It included pictures of Earl and Homer, two of the multiple victims 'found dead at the scene.' There was a brief criminal history of both of them – Zeb was shocked to see how far over his head he'd been in the van in front of the stash house, and twisted with shame when he remembered how light-heartedly he'd called them 'Darrell-and-Darrell.' *They stayed and took the bullets while you were running.*

The other two dead men, the story said, were still unidentified. There was a survivor of the shooting who had escaped from the rescue van carrying him to the hospital. He was still at large and there was a number to call if the reader had any information that might help. *Jeez, Robin, you really kicked the hornet's nest this time.* Zeb read every word of the story twice without finding one word about himself.

He felt as if he'd crossed over some kind of a bridge he

hadn't even known was there. He had sat in a van on Monday with those men in the pictures and now they were dead. And Robin was on the run and would have to stay that way, now, forever. It gave him a queasy, dislocated feeling, knowing there would always be something in his life, now, that he would have to hide. *And that's if I'm lucky.* The skin of his arms grew goose pimples when he realized how much of the rest of his life was going to be thanks to luck. Well, and cowardice. Let's not forget how much I owe to that.

While Doris was still napping he brought in his box and unpacked, took a shower, shaved. Clean clothes felt luxurious to him now. He looked pretty good, in fact, except for his hair. He'd thought this was such a classy cut when the girl in the Unisex shop talked him into it but now, three weeks later, it was already too long. Justin Bieber looked tousled, but never shaggy – how did he do that? He must get it cut every couple of weeks. Zeb knew he couldn't afford a high-style haircut twice a month on a handyman's cash flow. I'll find a regular barber, he thought, and get it cut really short.

He bundled his dirty clothes and put them in the empty box, thinking that laundry was the next thing he'd have to negotiate. He came out into the kitchen feeling a little awkward about his cleaned-up appearance, but Doris didn't even look at him. She was on the phone, saying, 'Good! We'll do that.' When she hung up she told him, 'Eddy's got my spare tire repaired.' She handed him the keys. 'Would you run the car down there so he can put it back in that well where it belongs?'

He drove the two blocks carefully, thinking she knew where her spare tire was, she just didn't want to talk about it. He parked alongside the station and waited while Eddy brought the tire out and bolted it in the well.

Standing behind the car he realized suddenly that the person gassing up at one of the pumps was his sister. He hadn't thought of her since she threw him out, had forgotten he was still in her neighborhood. She turned from the pump and met his eyes by accident, reacted with open-mouthed shock and turned away. *OK, Jan, don't say hello. But you don't own the whole neighborhood, so just ease up on the outrage.*

When he got back to the mobile-home park Doris was on

the phone again, having what sounded like a nice civilized chat with somebody who was not family. He'd never thought about it before but you could tell the difference by the lack of heat. When she hung up she said, 'That was Betty Lou Tolliver, one of my neighbors here in the park. She used to have a big shop but she's retired now – she just takes a few customers in her house.'

'Doing what?' Zeb asked her, just to kill time, not caring.

'She's a beautician. She says she has a kitchen blind that needs its pull cord replaced, and she was wondering if you'd like to trade that job for a haircut.'

He had to turn away, pretend to check his shoelace, to hide his smile. Their tentative deal wasn't more than a couple of hours old and already she was shopping him around the neighborhood. *She wants me to stay.*

He wanted to tell her she had the makings of a great pimp, but he just said, 'I haven't done a whole lot of pull cords but I'll see what I can do.'

FOURTEEN

'Two o'clock already,' Sarah said. 'What's next? Where were we before we became media stars?'

'This is what's next,' Delaney said, walking out of his office with a message in his hands. 'Can you believe it? AFIS actually got a match on a print.' It was so rare that a lifted print was good enough – every time anybody expressed the hope for a match somebody said, 'In the movies.'

'A print from the house in Midvale Park?'

'From that carpet cleaner's van. Off the passenger's-side door, they said.'

'You think it could be – well, I guess it could be just about anybody's, couldn't it?'

'Could be, sure. But the match is to a DUI arrest four months ago. Right here in Tucson. The guy's name is, get this' – he read off his note – 'Zebulon Montgomery Butts.'

'No fooling – for real?'

'Sounds like a joke but it's what's on the record.'

'How do we know he's connected to our case?'

'We don't yet. But there's a Tucson address. We can pick him up as a person of interest and see what else he matches.'

'That's all that's in the record, one DUI?'

'All they found, yeah. I know, big jump from there to home invasion. But . . . the house at his last address has a phone number in the name of Luella M. Butts. I called it and got no answer, but it's a working phone. I was just coming out to see – if you've got time why don't you get somebody to go with you? If you find him you can bring him in.'

She found Ollie in his work space. 'I'm getting ready to go interview Luella Butts, you want to go along?'

'God, yes,' Ollie said. 'Who's Luella Butts?'

'Probably some relative of Zebulon Montgomery Butts, whose print we lifted off the carpet cleaner's van.'

'And if Luella is his mother we want to ask her why she names her children after well-known historical figures?'

'That, and he got a DUI four months ago that the print matches, so Delaney thinks we should bring him in for questioning.' He wasn't standing up yet so she said, 'You can be the one who holds up the picture of the running man – won't that be fun?'

'What the hay,' Ollie said, getting up. 'It's a chance to get out of the building and ride with a major babe who spent the morning pawing over dead bodies.'

'Oh, Ollie, it's so swell to have a pal who shares my interests.'

On the way they talked about the photo op they'd just been to. Ollie said, 'Did you know Delaney could smile like that?'

'No. And the chief going on about fine team work – first he heard about that house was when we brought him the cash.'

'It makes a good story, though.'

'Sure. The stories always look as if we're winning.'

'Why do you hate them so much? It's just the standard drill.'

'It seems so *Keystone Kops*, posing for a picture. With all the guns and money on a table, us standing behind, grinning like trained apes.'

'Hey, take a breath. The chief needs to show results. If he can get the city council to refrain from cutting our budget any further we might even hang onto our jobs.' He treated her to a cheery gap-toothed grin. 'Besides, there won't be any more pictures now till we catch the ex-dead-guy, which will apparently be never. Looks to me like he's too quick and clever to get caught.'

'He's not. I'm with Delaney on this one – in the end, we're going to get that guy. Is this the place?' Luella Butts lived in a courtyard full of stucco casitas, four to a unit, with small balconies. Tiny gardens by the front doors held a cactus, a clay pot, and cutesy figurines, mostly howling coyotes with neck scarves and geese in bonnets.

Luella Butts opened the inner door as soon as they rang, watched them hold up their shields and heard them identify themselves. She unlocked the outer wire-mesh door finally and said, 'Come in.' Her voice was guarded: not friendly, not quite combative either. Doing what I have to do as usual, her face said.

She confirmed that she was Luella Butts, so Sarah asked her, 'Are you related to Zebulon Montgomery Butts?'

'He's my son. What about him? He doesn't live here any more.'

Ollie showed her the picture that Barney Gross had taken Monday from the car. 'Is this him?'

Her face was firmly set, stoical, but as she looked at the picture a nerve jumped in her cheek. Then her mouth went slack and began to tremble, and her eyes, looking up at Ollie, shone with tears. 'Why's he running?'

'We don't know,' Ollie said.

'Was somebody chasing him?'

'No. He was running away from a crime scene that he may or may not have been involved in, and we want to talk to him.' He leaned a little toward her, let his voice go soft. 'He's a person of interest, that's all. If you can tell us where to find him, we may be able to clear this right up.'

Sarah watched him anxiously, afraid he might disappear entirely into his good-cop persona and tell Luella Butts she had nothing to worry about. But he pulled back from the edge of that precipice, got out his notebook and stood waiting, pen in hand.

'I don't know.' She started with the simple declarative, immediately felt it was inadequate, and said again, plaintively, 'I don't *know*.'

She did a full parental meltdown in front of them then, within a three-foot-square space in her living room. Huffed and shrugged, turned, turned back, and said, 'My son is . . .' Sighed gustily and threw her arms out with the palms up. 'My son is having trouble finding himself.' She looked at Sarah, saw something in her face she evidently took to be understanding and said quickly, 'So I put his things outside my door and told him to continue the search on his own.'

Sarah said, 'Where did he go to start?' and thought about her sister Janine and some of the places she had gone. Janine had been looking for herself for so long now it seemed as if the search must have become the destination. Sarah understood Zebulon's mother very well and had no helpful suggestions.

'My daughter let him sleep at her place for a while.' Luella Butts shook her head, grieving. 'She works the same shift as I do at the hospital and when she told me about it I said, "Baby, that's a mistake." I said, "What's the use me doing tough love and then you take up the slack?" But she said, "Mom, we can't have him sleeping in the park with bums." Well, I'd already thought about that; she ought to know I would think about that plenty. But the young always think they know better. She learned soon enough I was right. Before long he did what he always does.'

'What's that?'

'Takes advantage. Can't be satisfied with what you offer, has to have more. Messed her place up – after she warned him!' Luella Butts was twisting her hands together now. 'So in the end she threw him out, too.'

Sarah said, 'Where'd he go from there?'

'Janet says she doesn't know and she doesn't want to know. "Just keep him away from me," she said. How am I supposed to do that when I don't know where he is? But Zeb does that to people, makes them so frustrated – it's like he can't see past the end of his own nose sometimes. What kind of a crime scene?' she asked Ollie suddenly.

'The one that's in the paper, the home invasion with the shooting.'

'Omigod.' She clutched her chest. 'Are you saying Zeb was there? Is that where you took this picture?'

'Not at the house,' Ollie said. 'He was running on a street a couple of blocks from there and—'

'Well, then, you don't really know he had anything to do with it, do you?'

'No. He's just a person of interest at this time. If you could tell me where to find him—'

'Was that a drug deal gone bad?' Luella asked him, rolling out her *CSI* jargon.

'Well, uh, I'm sorry, I'm afraid I can't . . . we aren't free to release details until I find him and talk to him.' Ollie hardly ever used official cant, and when he did he sounded embarrassed. Luella Butts took his embarrassment as an admission of dishonesty and pounced on it.

'Now see here,' she said, 'I pay plenty of taxes, I hold up my end, and I don't have to put up with this.' She had been carrying a lot of anger around for a long time and Ollie was standing right in the path of it now. 'You come here to my house, two of you with guns and badges, probably get all my neighbors asking me questions, talking about me behind my back. And now you can't give me any details? What kind of bullshit is that?'

'We're not playing tricks on you, Mrs Butts,' Sarah said. 'We just need to talk to Zebulon.'

'I'll bet it's got something to do with that sneaky kid named Robin that's always getting Zeb to come help him with something. Am I right? Thinks he's so smart, that guy. But he's no good for anything but causing trouble.'

'I honestly don't know if he's involved,' Ollie said. 'Do you know where I can find Robin?'

'No, I don't. And why should I tell you if I did? You can't tell *me* anything *I* need to know, can you? So why don't you just get the hell out? Go on and leave me alone.' They did their best to reason with her, offered her their cards in case she . . . 'Forget that, I won't call you. I don't want to see you again ever!' she yelled. She was in a rage now, all stops out and enjoying the release. 'Never around when I need you, let me get run over on the street by these crazies going through red lights, and then you come here in my own house and bother me? Just get out!' She threw open the door and stood in it, pointing. As she had predicted, a couple of neighbors had come out to watch.

Finally they gave it up and started back to the car. When they were halfway down the walk she leaned out of her door and shouted after them: 'You better not hurt him when you do find him. You hear me?'

Ollie said, driving away, 'Sure wish we got the daughter's address before she blew.'

'I bet I can find her anyway. Didn't Luella say her name was Janet? And she didn't mention a son-in-law. Janet's last name's probably still Butts. Pull over in this patch of shade and I'll research her.' Pictures were already dancing on her small screen. 'Same shift at Carondolet as Mama, that's what she said, right?

'Yes.' Watching her work, he said, 'Wish I had a smarter phone.'

'Why don't you?'

'All those daughters.'

'Come on, you only have two.'

'They seem like more. So many needs.'

'OK, I've got her. Janet Butts, she's an admissions clerk at Carondolet.'

'Young girls are like alien life forms invading a swamp, you know?' Ollie's big hands curled into claws. 'Spreading unchecked, growing and changing . . .' Sarah had heard Ollie's family rant so often she knew parts of it by heart. She went on searching, found Janet Butts on Facebook and LinkedIn. By the time he got to the part about special shampoos and slumber parties she had email and street addresses. 'No phone number yet but come on, let's go there and find her.'

'Probably just get yelled at again,' Ollie said.

'So what? Sometimes they yell something useful.'

'Especially when they're family,' Ollie said. 'Don't get me started on families.'

'I won't.' She gave him the address and in a few minutes she said, 'I think it's that big apartment complex up ahead there, behind the bus stop.'

Janet Butts was home and let them in reluctantly. She didn't shed any tears over the picture, just nodded and handed it back to Sarah.

'That's your brother?'

'Yes. Are you going to arrest him?'

'We just want to talk to him,' Ollie said. 'When did you see him last?'

'Tuesday morning. Early, about six o'clock, when I threw him out of here and told him never to come back.'

'He made you mad, huh?'

'Yes, he did.'

'What did he do?'

She drew a shaky breath. 'He didn't stay in the laundry room where he belonged.'

'He belongs in the laundry? How come?'

'Because he . . .' She began to pace. 'When he comes out he cooks my food, sits in my chair . . .' Sarah and Ollie watched her, waiting to hear the bad part. She blew up suddenly like her mother, yelling, 'See, that's the infuriating thing about Zeb: when I say what he does wrong it makes me sound so petty! Because I can never explain how with him it's always one little thing after a hundred other little things, and—' Breathing hard, she gave it up. 'Hopeless,' she muttered.

Ollie said, 'So . . . you haven't seen him since Tuesday morning?'

'No. I mean, not to talk to.'

Four detectives' eyes fastened on her like magnets on metal. Sarah said, 'Not to talk to, but you did see him?'

'At the gas station. And that's infuriating too – what's he doing, getting a car serviced in my neighborhood? He doesn't live here!'

'We don't know,' Ollie said. 'We were kind of hoping you'd tell us.'

'I have no idea.' She shrugged, walked around some more, shrugged again. Zeb seemed to be the kind of a guy who made women pace and shrug. 'But that old car – I've seen it around here before with somebody else driving it.'

'Who?'

'I can't remember!' She tossed her hair back, combed it with her fingers.

'Tell us about the car,' Sarah said. Janet looked puzzled. 'Can you describe it?'

'Well . . . I don't . . . it's gray. Kind of old-looking.'

'Two doors or four?'

'Wow, I don't know. Just . . . kind of square and stodgy . . . like that thing they say . . . your father's,' she flapped her hands, 'whatever.'

'It's an Oldsmobile?'

'No. Um . . . I want to say Buick. Mom had a Buick for a while and seems to me it was square like that and had a logo like, kind of . . . shields?'

'Very good,' Ollie said, encouraging. 'But you can't describe the person who was driving it before?'

'No. I can't remember. Isn't that crazy? But soon as I saw Zeb standing by it, I thought, what's he doing with *that* car?'

'Tell you what,' Sarah said, handing her a card, 'if you see that car or your brother again, will you call me?'

Janet looked at the card but didn't take it. 'I don't want to get involved in anything that's going on with Zeb.'

'You won't. Just make the phone call and we'll take it from there.'

'I know you mean well,' Janet said, 'but you don't understand how hard it is to not get involved with a screw-up like my brother.'

In the end she took the card. But Sarah said, as they drove away, 'I bet she throws it away as soon as we're out of sight.'

'I'm beginning to want to meet this guy,' Ollie said.

'Me, too,' Sarah said. 'Those are two very frustrated women. But they can't seem to explain why, can they?'

'No. But . . . a screw-up, they say . . . he doesn't sound like a murderer, does he?'

'No,' Sarah said, 'he sounds like a mope who makes women crazy. And all that screaming, coming after three autopsies . . . please say it's quitting time.'

'OK,' Ollie said, heading back to the station. 'It's quitting time.'

'I've never been that crazy about Wednesdays, anyway,' Sarah said, waxing irrational because fatigue was swamping her, 'and today I'm trapped in one that's determined to go on forever.'

'I'm with you all the way on this issue,' Ollie said. 'We'll start a Hate Wednesday club; I bet everybody will join.'

Turning in at her house an hour later, though, the big trees all in fresh leaf, mockingbirds noisy in the high branches, and the good smell of something with beef and tomatoes, she left the department behind. She'd had her doubts about moving the four of them into this house together – *My mother, my niece and my boyfriend? Sounds like a French farce.* But Will had convinced her it was the only way they'd ever have any time together. And bless him, bless everybody, so far it was working better than she'd dared to expect. They were getting used to the house and each other, each finding their favorite spots to be alone in and the best places to talk when they felt gabby.

Denny ran out the door as she parked, grinning and waving a piece of paper. The second the car stopped she yanked open the driver's-side door and yelled, 'I got A's in English and Math both, and Gram's teaching me how to make lasagna!'

'Well, hey, a better than average day, huh? Come in with me while I change and show me that beautiful report card.'

In the master bedroom she locked away her shield and service weapon and got into soft clothes. Denny danced around her, showing off the good grades and telling her the rest of it, 'The really super part.' Mr Carson, the math teacher, had kept Denny and two other students after class. 'We were all like, oh, wow, what did we do wrong?'

But no, he wanted to tell them that since they all had near-perfect scores for three months running they were eligible to apply for a grant-sponsored math camp this summer. 'Two weeks in the White Mountains and it's free and he'll help us fill out the forms, so can I go? Please, please, please?'

'Of course you can go, if – I mean, is there something that tells parents who the supervisors are? And do you live in tents or . . . And who cooks?'

Denny said, 'There's a brochure, what did I do with it? Oh, rats, it's in my backpack.' She started out the door.

'Wait,' Sarah said. If it was in Denny's backpack they might never see it again. A low-level argument about the weighty clutter in Denny's backpack had been going on all year but right now she didn't want it to spoil the good mood the kid had earned.

'Take your time – find it while I see if I can help Mom with dinner. I'm so proud of you; let's have a hug.' They treated each other to a big, rocking-and-patting embrace. 'Now after all that praise you ought to be strong enough to sort out your backpack.'

Denny made a face and cried out, 'Truly, Watson, there are times when the extraordinary demands of my vocation are daunting! I must go back to Baker Street and continue my research!' She staggered into her room, clutching her heart.

Sarah walked into the kitchen and told her mother, 'Maybe I overdid it, giving her the whole collection of Sherlock Holmes.'

'Better for her vocabulary than *Little Women*,' Aggie said. 'At least she's quit calling me Marmee.' She was sitting on a high stool spinning salad greens in a drying bowl. 'You're home for dinner two nights in a row. Any chance this will start a trend?'

'I hope. Can I finish the salad?'

'Sure. Pull up the other stool. Veggies there in the crisper.' As Sarah chopped she said, 'Denny tell you about the math camp?'

'Did she ever. She's so excited. You think it sounds OK?'

'Oh, it *sounds* wonderful. I guess to make sure we'll have to go over to the school and eyeball that teacher.'

'You don't think he's—'

'I haven't heard anything to make me dubious. But I don't want to sit here in July and worry about it.'

'For sure. I'd like to meet the counselors, too, and some of the parents of kids who've gone to it before. Do you think,' Sarah threw cucumber slices on top of the lettuce, 'if more people understood that parenting is just one worrying fit after another, the birth rate would be lower?'

Aggie made a small ironic sound. 'Probably not. We all think we're going to be that one perfect person who can pull it off without a hitch.'

FIFTEEN

Monday night and Tuesday were easy – Robin was so pumped about the slick way he got away from the rescue squad that he hardly needed any sleep that first night. Same with food; he bought a couple of snacks out of a vending machine before he left the hospital and ate them while he strolled the first three floors of the parking garage, scoping out the darkest corners. He found the best vantage points that first night, too, places where he could see people coming from any direction. They were all bright places, though, so he could never pause in any of them for long. Traffic was brisk for the first few hours; drivers busy parking their cars or finding them. All he had to do was keep moving and nobody paid any attention to him.

After ten it slowed down, just night shift people going and coming, so he had less traffic to dodge but a greater risk of exposure to the few people he met. He spent some time sitting in his dark spots, then began to like the stairwell after he noticed how few others used it – even for one flight, people all took the elevator. It got pretty cold on the stairs after midnight, though, so he stole a tarp from the bed of a pickup. Wrapped up, he had a nice late-night snooze between third and fourth floors. Prison had taught him to sleep lightly and wake at any nearby sound.

That wasn't the only useful skill Robin had learned in the Arizona State Prison system. He had gone in there thoroughly schooled, he thought, by the street where he mostly grew up, and by his times in juvie and Pima County. But Wilmot Road showed him that what he had thought were his best assets – a slender, attractive figure, a smart mouth and a pretty face – were the worst possible combination to bring with you into state lockup.

He had always been a quick study and pain speeded up his learning curve. In a couple of months he had come to the stunning realization that he was likely to get out of Wilmot, if at all, with fewer teeth and a sexually transmitted disease.

He had been sitting in the dining room, just out of the infirmary for the second time and wondering if he had the guts to commit suicide, when a fortyish man with caramel skin and a graying Van Dyke had sat down beside him and said, 'You just about ready to listen to reason?'

His name was Regis Boe. A lifer whose attorney had beaten the death sentence he had well and truly earned, he led a gang of the most fearsome badasses in Wilmot prison. Not the crazies, but the cold-eyed dealers, men who understood that life on the inside could be almost as good as life on the outside if you played it right. You had to know which ones to bribe and who had to be terrified instead. Then you lined up the pleasures you wanted and fixed it so somebody else paid for them.

He had decided to make Robin his new special boyfriend. His standard practice was to take his pick of the freshest young things that came in, let some of his boys break them in first and then present himself as the road to rescue. Robin had already been through the first part of the process and was as ready for a rescue as he needed to be. They could do it the easy way or the hard way, Regis explained, and Robin chose the easy way without even asking for specifics.

There were really no surprises, anyway. He became an adroit sex slave, skilled at giving pleasure. He never learned to enjoy any of it himself, so the anger of the forlorn, neglected child he had been, that in his teens had built him into a tricky thief and a mean bully, now became a raging hunger that fed on inflicting pain.

Regis felt his anger, saw how quick and bright Robin was, and put his martial arts teachers to work. He had plenty of amusements and enjoyed them all, but he was a true psychopath and now he began to enjoy watching his acolytes turn Robin into a lightning-fast fighting machine. There was plenty of exercise time allowed in Wilmot, and with good behavior – a joke in this context but once Robin was under Regis's wing he could pick his fights and the rules called his new silence good behavior – he could get extra time in the weight room and the yard. He took all the exercise time he could get and bulked up a little. Whenever Regis wanted somebody punished, Robin was his man.

It was Owen Chu, the tiny lifer who'd killed his wife for cheating – he made her watch him kill both their children first – who taught Robin how to control his breathing and pulse rate. Owen had days when he didn't make much sense, so most people didn't want to be around him. But Robin noticed how nimble and strong he was, so he ignored Owen's rants and got acquainted with his workout routines.

The breathing- and muscle-control exercises that Chu and the other martial arts guys taught him could be practiced in small spaces, even alone in his cell in the dark. He learned to take himself to the edge of unconsciousness, to achieve trance-like states in which his pulse rate dropped to near zero. He loved the feeling of control, especially after Chu said, 'Forget all that crap about Hindu gods – you don't have to be a mystic to make this work.' A practical path to power, Chu called it. It was hard to see any path to power opening up for Chu, walled up in Wilmot, but Robin saw right away how he could use it.

When he got out and started making his living on the street again, he was delighted to see that the speed and ruthlessness he had learned in prison gave him a great advantage over ordinary men. He went on practicing on the outside, improving his ability to always make the first kick or grab and follow at once with a second devastating blow while his opponent was still reeling.

And the day of the invasion, his ability to control his breathing and metabolism had given him the crucial edge. He congratulated himself on these skills now. The knowledge that he had put one over on the Tucson Police Department, fooled them in the house and caught them flat-footed in the rescue vehicle, warmed him through the long night in the parking garage, kept him dreaming that the big prize might still be his.

His tiny radio fit easily in the breast pocket of his fire depart-ment shirt. He felt pretty secure, strolling through the cars with the earbuds in – they made him look relaxed, he thought, and ensured that nobody would talk to him. All the local stations were broadcasting bulletins about the 'multiple slayings in Midvale Park,' and 'the lone survivor.' He imagined himself telling Regis, with a little wink, 'That's how I knew I was still at large.'

They kept reporting a home invasion, and saying 'multiple victims' but not how many – the police still weren't releasing details, like the fact that the home was a stash house. And they hadn't said a word about the money. Which meant what – they hadn't found it, or they had? Thinking about the money in somebody else's hands made his chest ache with anger. It was his; he had earned it!

The front part of the invasion had gone exactly as he planned – he knew Earl and Homer, those idiots, would buy his idea about a service van being the perfect cover, and if anything he'd expected the bald guy inside to be a little quicker with the Desert Eagle. *But hey, Rolly's jolly.* That used to be his thing to say in the olden days – three whole years ago, before he got busted. Rolly had been his gang name for a couple of years. It made Rolly very jolly now to know that all four of those bozos were dead. There was nobody left, now, to talk about the house on Spring Brook Drive. Except, just possibly, silly old Zeb.

The back of the house – his part – had been a huge, stellar success. He went over it again in his mind, proud of the bold way he went through the window, created one of his tiny pockets of time and got his Derringer into perfect position to fire one killing shot into the brain of the man with the Kalashnikov, who by the way was showing a lot of class himself planted in the doorway like that, fearlessly laying down a field of fire. Almost a shame to waste a guy like that.

The real clinker in the bunch of course had been Zeb, who as far as Robin could tell had never made it into the house at all. Infuriating, but not surprising. He had only ever needed Zeb to help with the window. After that, one way or another, Zeb was slated to get blown away – if the house guards didn't get him Robin would have to. You couldn't have a dickhead like Zeb around afterward, with his mouth and his yeah-buts.

The whole first night Robin kept waiting for one of the newscasters to report one man in custody. When nobody did he began to think the unthinkable – that Zeb, the stupid dork, must have succeeded in running away. That was better than Zeb in custody, telling everything he knew, but if he was still out there, he was one more thing Robin needed to take care of before he could run.

And, oh damn, he was so ready to run. He was going to get himself out to LA, where it was easy to become somebody else, and get some fake ID for a new name. Make some contacts there and in San Diego while he changed his appearance a little – maybe grow a beard? He'd been Richard and Rolly and Robin, and nobody had ever cared for any of those boys except to use and abuse. So now he would be somebody else and he would do the using and abusing. He'd have money, which bought time, and he would use the time to get a new identity and build a new face.

When the time was right his new self would come right back to Tucson, though. Arizona was still the best place for him, where he knew the best ways to cross the border, where to go to make deals. He didn't want to get into drug-smuggling itself, no point in bumping asses with the big cartels. He was going to become the go-to guy for all the adjunct services the drug trade required: the guns, cars, houses, and electronics. He hadn't worked out all the details yet but he knew the most important part – his new business would be built around the border; the gift that kept on giving, the magic line where the price went up.

Thinking that way, keeping a positive outlook as long as he could and controlling his breathing whenever anger threatened to swamp him, he handled Tuesday and Tuesday night very well. Trips for more supplies were risky: eating and drinking required more trips to a bathroom, so despite his restless need to break up the boredom he resisted hunger and thirst as much as he could. It helped that after two nights and a day he could hardly stand the sight of vending machine food.

He had a bad moment when he noticed a nurses' aide watching him thoughtfully and realized she looked familiar to him, too – yellow braid, always parked on the second floor.

He scooted up a stairwell, got in the darkest corner on Three and used his breathing to zone out for a while. When he came out of that trance he toured Children's Hospital till he found a set of scrubs to change into. They served him well till he was almost ready to leave. By then he had located a set of lockers that yielded a pair of shorts and a T-shirt that were a loose fit, good to hide things under.

So he was surviving very well, but he needed to get out of this parking garage, get his money and go. The hold-up was that he had never been able to determine, listening to the radio, if the detectives were still working on the house on Spring Brook Drive. Little dribbles of information kept leaking out – it was definitely four bodies now, and they were seeking, always seeking, the escapee from the rescue vehicle and 'another person of interest.' Had Zeb been spotted running away? Who else could it be?

On Wednesday afternoon, the newscasts reported the release of new information from the Tucson Police Department. The multiple shootings on Spring Brook Drive were revealed as 'a drug-related crime.' The home was a stash house and the investigation had yielded a 'high-value seizure' of the house: SUV, drugs . . . and oh, God, money . . . upwards of a quarter of a million dollars in money, they said, and drugs with an estimated street value of about the same amount.

Robin didn't hear the value of the drugs because he had pulled the earbuds out of his ears and was crouched in the darkest of his dark places with his head between his knees, practicing the rapid breathing Owen had taught him to ward off nausea.

Those dirty bastards had his money! For a few minutes his brain wouldn't do any useful work at all – it was too busy building a wall of denial: *It can't be can't be can't be.*

A small, sneaky part of his mind, a remnant from his childhood, kept trying to claw its way back to yesterday and try for a do-over.

He was still Robin Brady, though, so even in his agony he heard footsteps coming closer to his part of the ramp and realized he had to get up and move. Moving got his synapses firing and soon he was thinking as he trotted up the empty

stairwell to the next level, *They didn't say anything about
the skim.* Of course this was young reporters writing news
stories transmitted to them by dorky cops who thought like
eagle scouts. They probably wouldn't think to look for the
skim . . . *I bet I can still get that part of the money.* OK, it
was a lot less money than he'd planned to have, but it was
still a lot more than he had right now.

Robin knew he could only boost one car in this location.
After that, cops would be all over this garage with dogs and
technicians. When he snatched his wheels, he had to be ready
to grab the money and go. He'd even picked the car he wanted
– a last year's Taurus with Michelin tires, that a young doc,
kind of a babe actually, parked on Three every morning before
she hustled her cute little butt into Children's Hospital for the
nine-to-six shift. A white sedan that looked like every third
car in Tucson, and she kept plenty of gas in the tank – he'd
been watching it, was beginning to like it a lot. He'd have
nine hours in it before she even came out and found it missing
– by then he could have driven it to Yuma, switched it for
something else in a parking lot, and gone on his way.

Every hour of Wednesday and Wednesday night felt like
three – sometimes he was sure his watch had stopped.
Newscasts about the slayings on Spring Brook Drive were
getting shorter and harder to find – Tucson was moving on.
He used his breathing to keep himself quiet until Thursday
morning, when he knew if he ate another cardboard sandwich
he'd kill somebody. This was it – his day to run.

He watched the sun coming up. Feeling his pulse beat,
knowing this was his day at last. But 8:45 came, then 9:00,
and his Taurus didn't show. The cute little doc was late to
work. Or could it be her day off? No way to know. He jittered
between the two possible alternates he had picked, not sure
which steering column would be easier to crack. And then,
oh, hot shit, here she was, squealing the brakes on the corners,
wheeling into her spot. Grabbed her kit, slammed the door
and ran across the ramp, swearing under her breath.

And the rest of the heist went exactly as he had planned.
The screwdriver he'd lifted out of a janitor's closet in the
hospital slid into the slot and cracked the disks. The motor

roared to life and he was out of the parking slot and down the ramp. Driving south on Campbell Avenue toward the money, he sang a little tuneless march under his breath, *Tada rump-ump-ump, tada rada dah dah!* It was the action song he and his gang used to sing on Oklahoma Street back in the day when he was Rolly, before he'd been split off from himself and the top half, the part he let people see, went back to being Robin.

Sometimes he still let himself remember how much fun that gang had been, ready for anything. After they tuned up on some nice weed, before they headed out to spray paint a wall, boost a car, whatever, he'd sing out, 'Hey, Rolly's jolly! Let's go do it!' And they would jump into the cars and sing that silly marching song all the way to the caper.

SIXTEEN

'Sarah,' Ray Menendez said. 'Can I talk to you?'

'Sure.' She typed another whole sentence while she waited for him to start. When he didn't she said, 'What?'

'I got a problem.'

'What?' She turned to look at him finally and found herself staring at his belt buckle. He was standing very close to her desk, talking softly to the top of her ear. She stood up, looked straight into his eyes and said, 'What's wrong with you and why are we whispering about it?'

'I can't find my radio.' He was still mumbling.

'Why tell me? It's probably in your car.'

'I looked in my car. Several times. Also in my house, and all the drawers in my desk. I've pulled everything out of my briefcase twice.'

'I still don't— Can we please sit down?' Watching him wring his hands in front of her desk she said, 'Can you remember when you saw it last?'

'Tuesday morning, shortly after two.'

'You mean in the house in Midvale Park?'

'That's where we were. Yes.'

'Oh, crud.'

'I had it when we started looking for the money.' he said. 'I remember setting it down on a closet shelf in the bedroom so I could turn over a chair. After that . . .' He made one frantic attempt at self-justification. 'We were all so tired!'

'I know.' It didn't change anything. 'When did you notice it was missing?'

Ray shrugged helplessly. 'I never even thought about it Tuesday afternoon, I was too – you know how we all were: walking dead. But I've been looking for it steady since yesterday morning. I'm sure it's in that house.' He rocked in her spare chair, his face a mask of misery. 'Delaney's going to kill me.'

'Oh, come on, it's not that bad.' It was, though. A department radio, out in the world lost, breached all communications. If they couldn't find it they'd have to re-key . . . She couldn't even finish the thought. 'We just have to go down there and . . .' She stopped, took a breath. 'We just have to get a judge to reinstate the search warrant and then go down there and . . .' They looked at each other for a few seconds. Then they both stood up and walked toward Delaney's office. 'You explain your problem,' Sarah said. 'I'll sell him on the answer.'

The first two minutes went well. Delaney walked out the door of his office as they walked up to it, closed his phone and stopped in front of them looking . . . not excited – Delaney didn't do excited – but . . . pleased.

'I just got a call from Phil Cruz at the DEA,' he said. 'The paper called him to ask if he had any comment on the drugs-and-money story, and he's interested to hear more details of how that went down. I told him you were primary on the case, Sarah, and he asked if you could come down for a chat. You know him, right? So will you give him a call and set something up?'

'Sure. But before I do that, boss,' Sarah said, 'Ray's got a problem and we need your OK to go fix it.'

The next five minutes were not much more painful than a root canal, Ray said later. They were safely out of the building by then, with their renewed warrant, headed toward the house in Midvale Park. Sarah had accepted Delaney's logic, that if she was going to ask a judge to reopen a search warrant on a crime scene, which she pretty much had to do, goddammit, owing to the boneheaded carelessness of this poor excuse for a detective here, she had better damn well go along and preserve the integrity of the evidence. Because if any of this came back to bite them later at trial . . . his phone had been blinking with another call for some time and he let the threat hang in the air, waved them away and answered it.

The Midvale Park neighborhood had the dead quiet of a block where all the parents worked, and children who weren't in school got carried to grandmothers and sitters. In the park two blocks from Spring Brook Drive, the merry-go-round was silent and the empty swings were still. There was already graffiti on the raw boards that blocked the windows of the crime scene house – one more blight in an already struggling block. An absentee landlord wasn't answering phone calls or messages, Sarah knew. The SUV had been towed from the garage, and papers filed for the forfeit of house and car.

'Gloves and booties,' Sarah said, pulling forward a box of both. They put them on in the car. Sarah found a small manila envelope in her purse and shook out a ring of keys. 'Let's see, two locks,' she said, and isolated the ones for the front door.

'If my radio's not here I'm going to open a vein,' Ray said.

'Not on this property you don't,' Sarah said. 'I've seen enough of this place to last me forever. Let's do this quick and quiet and be gone before anybody knows we're here.' Her brain kept composing a scenario in which somebody tipped a reporter, who arrived with a photographer in time to do a story on sloppy police work.

The flags and tape, all the litter of the crime scene had been cleared away. A stained front step and the scars from bullet removal were the only reminders of a crime scene. Sarah turned the two keys and Ray opened the door and pushed past her, impatient. Coming in from bright sunshine Sarah was blind for a few seconds and stood still, pulling the door shut behind her. The house was dark, drapes drawn, power turned off. The disgusting smell was fainter, but still there.

She followed him across the stained floor, along the hall that turned a corner to the bedrooms. In the second one he pulled open the closet door, peered along a shelf and said, 'Hah!' He came out holding a radio, with his patented Latin-lover smile at full gleam. 'Oh, baby,' he said, kissing it, 'I love you so much.'

'Well, good,' she said. 'Now we can— What?' He had set the radio back on the shelf, crossed the two steps between them and grabbed her. Shushing her with his finger on his lips, he pulled her back toward the closet.

'Saw somebody . . . edge of the window.' His whisper was so quiet, she barely heard. She looked, saw nothing but window, turned her head an inch toward him with a tiny shake. Wordless, he pointed toward the window and tugged her toward it. As she got closer to the wall, suddenly she saw it.

On the outside, a knot had fallen out of the cheap lumber boarding up the window. In here, there was a half-inch gap between the venetian blind and the wall. If she stood on tiptoe she could see most of the backyard through the hole in the board. Ray, stooping behind her, had almost the same view.

A young man was wriggling through a gap in the wooden fence at the far end of the yard. While they watched, he sucked up and got through, stood still a moment pulling a sliver out of his arm, and walked across the backyard toward the house. He passed right across the little hole and out of her line of sight.

Holding her breath, Sarah pulled on the cord that worked the blind, saw the slats turn silently. She eased right and got a fresh view. If he looked right at her he might see her, but he wasn't looking at the window. Curiously his head was turned toward the standpipe behind the dying cactus. Why would a service man be squeezing through a hole in the fence? Wait – he straightened and her heart gave a jump. He was cleaned up and in different clothes, but his face was the unforgettable face that had looked up at her from under a bloody corpse in the room behind her three days ago, asking who she was.

She tugged on Ray's sleeve and whispered, 'Ex-Dead-Guy!'

'Wait.' His whisper had hardly any breath behind it now, was almost as quiet as thought. 'See what he does . . .'

The man bent toward the control box set into the ground beside the standpipe. It looked the way all outdoor control boxes looked, had the standard beige plastic cover with an etched label that read, 'Irrigation Control Valve.' The man squatted by the box, reached under the edge of the plastic lid, got a grip on the cover and lifted it off.

As he was lifting the lid off the box, while he was still squatting, Sarah tugged Ray's sleeve, whispered, 'Now!' and sprinted for the front door, hearing Ray behind her. They had to go all the way around the front; the back was nailed shut. Ray had longer legs and pulled ahead. Sarah was right behind him, getting her Glock out, as they rounded the back corner of the house.

But he had heard them; he was gone. The cover lay beside

the box, upside down. Across the yard, a small board trembled by the hole in the fence where she had seen him enter the yard. They ran to it. Sarah squeezed through, heard Ray struggling behind her, hurling obscene threats at broken boards. In the next yard, a shirt on one of the clothes lines still swayed. She pelted past it toward the empty street, Ray pounding right behind her. On the sidewalk they whirled in circles, looking. There was no one in sight.

'How could he— Let's try that way,' Ray said, pointing east on Chardonnay.

'Go ahead,' Sarah said. 'I'll go get the car.' She ran back toward it, holstering her weapon, looking everywhere. She could see Ray's running figure in the rearview as she started the motor. Between them, out of a side street she hadn't been aware of, a late-model Taurus crossed Chardonnay and drove south. She squinted – could that be him? Something about the shape of the driver's head seemed right. She leaned on her horn, made a tire-squealing U-turn and barreled toward Ray. He stopped and turned back when he heard the horn but he was almost to Oak Tree Drive. She slid to a stop beside him, turned the siren on as he closed the door. She had turned the corner onto Oak Tree Drive and was racing south before he had his belt on.

'Get on the radio and call for help,' she said. 'I'll see if I can cut him off.' She hit the siren and floorboarded the gas pedal for a block, turned right on two wheels and looked both ways at the next two cross streets. There was no late-model Taurus in sight.

They rendezvoused with the two cars that came to help, gave them a quick description of car and driver. The three cars drove a twenty-block grid for a quarter of an hour before they gave up. Sarah pulled into a patch of shade and parked, feeling her heartbeat slow.

Ray sat with his hands hanging limp between his knees. The air in the car was heavy with the sullen silence of failure. Finally Ray said, 'Well, that was fun. But please, Sarah, can we go get my radio now?'

Sarah yelled at the top of her lungs, 'Oh, piss on your damn radio!' The outburst shocked them both so much they just

stared at each other for an echoing interval. Finally Sarah said,
'Oh, God, Ray, I can't believe I said that to you,' and in a
bizarre reaction to the stress and frustration of the last half
hour, simultaneously they began to laugh. The release was so
welcome they couldn't stop – they howled, roared, pounded
on their knees, giving vent to the craziness of this week in
their lives. Their hilarity fed on its own noise until it shook
the car.

Then, rather suddenly, the air went out of their silly balloon.
They came back to earth, shook their heads in embarrassment,
and got back to business. Sarah drove quietly back to the house
on Spring Brook Drive while Ray called the duty sergeant and
put out a Need to Locate notice with a good description of
the wanted man and a partial one of the vehicle – neither of
them had seen the license number. As he finished, Sarah parked
at the curb in front of the house and said, 'Let's leave your
radio where it is for a minute and see what's in that control
box he opened.'

She grabbed her briefcase because it had her camera in it
and led the way around the end of the house. Behind her, Ray
said, 'There's my lady with the babies, watching us out her
picture window. Josephina.'

'Pretend you can't see her.'

'Too late. We already waved. Josephina and I are buds,' he
said proudly. Knowing he had found his radio was such a
satisfaction he had already forgotten the man who got away
and was back to bragging about his street smarts.

They stood together in the dried-up yard, alongside the
dying cactus, and stared down at the open box. 'I don't get
it,' Ray said, 'It's a standard lash-up for outdoor watering
systems. Low-voltage lines coming in here from that timer on
the wall. They connect to this solenoid—'

'Right, and then these two wires go to the valve that controls
the flow on these two water lines. Same thing I've got at home.
But what's this mound of gravel doing beside the pipes?' She
pushed some of it aside. 'Something black here.' She scooped
up the rest of the gravel. 'What is it?'

'It's a cap,' Ray said, authoritatively.

'You don't say.'

'Yes. A screw-on cap for something that shouldn't be here, that I never saw before and can't explain.' He looked at her brightly. 'You got any fresh gloves on you? These are getting kind of ragged.'

'Of course,' Sarah said, 'all detectives carry gloves.' She patted her pockets, found a pair and handed them over. He put them on and tried the lid. 'Turns easy. Usual threading.' When he had the cap off he peered into a dark interior space. 'I guess hardly anybody keeps live snakes in jars underground, huh?'

'Let's see.' Sarah's smart phone had a small flashlight that made Ray mutter, 'Cool.' She held it above the jar's mouth, looked inside, moved the light a little and looked some more. 'I can't believe—' She turned an incandescent smile toward Ray and said, 'Can you say supercalifragilisticexpialidocious?'

'No. What is it?'

'I think we just found a little cut-out.'

'Oh, you mean for . . .'

'Yeah. Somebody's been skimming.'

She plunged her hand inside. When she pulled it out it was holding a heavy royal-blue plastic bank bag, stuffed full and zippered along the top. The legend on the side read, 'First National Bank of Baltimore, Maryland.'

Ray opened the zipper halfway, said, 'Oh, *yes*,' and closed it back up fast.

'Wait,' she said, and reached again. The second bag was gray, equally fat, and read, 'Farmer's State Bank of Ames, Iowa.'

'These people get around.'

'More,' she said, and brought out a bulging green one that said, 'Miners' Union Bank, Butte, Montana.' She felt around inside the jar. 'That's it.'

'OK,' Ray said, screwing the cap back on. 'Now can we grab my radio and get the hell out of here? Because I'm getting a dark brown feeling in the back of my throat.'

'Damn straight,' Sarah said, slamming the lid in place. 'I think I can get all three of these money sacks in my brief case. Oy vey, heavy now. Smile pretty when you wave to Josephina, please. Look as if you never heard the word money.'

'What kind of a look is that?'

'You know, light-hearted.'

'I'm a police detective. If I look light-hearted I'll get fired.'

At the front door, nervously jingling the house keys, she said, 'Show me how fast you can get a radio.' She felt as if every house in the block had a gun pointed at her.

He was back in thirty seconds that felt like half an hour, saying, 'You don't need the keys.' He set the lock from the inside and pulled the door shut. 'Let's go.'

In the car, halfway to the station, he said, 'I thought finding buried treasure was supposed to be fun. Why am I not having fun?'

'Because we're humble working folk and driving around with this much cash makes us feel guilty and furtive and threatened. Are you actually checking your weapon?'

'Yes, I am. Because when I feel guilty and furtive and threatened I like to make sure I'm carrying a full clip. Why are you driving five miles under the speed limit?'

'Because I've started to imagine we will have a traffic accident and the newspaper headline will read, "Two Tucson detectives found with hoard of cash in car."'

'Please, Sarah, speed up the damn car. It already feels like downtown got moved forty miles farther north of Midvale Park.'

'I know. But here's the bridge and South Stone is right over there – I'm starting to think this is going to be fun in just a few more minutes.'

'Curb your enthusiasm. Remember we work for a bureaucracy.'

Delaney was waiting for them as they came off the elevator. Ray had phoned him on the way back so he would hear from them first that the fugitive got away. 'I heard part of the chase. You're pretty sure you were after Robin Brady?'

'We know he was at the house when we were there. We think we almost caught him in a white Taurus, but— Can we go in your office, please? And close the door?'

Delaney looked at her as if she'd said something indecent but he walked into his office. They followed him in and closed the door.

'What, for God's sake?' he said. 'Did you wreck the car?'

'Boss, just . . . please. We . . . I need to sit.'

He made a despairing gesture. 'Who's stopping you? Sit.'

They all sat down and Sarah pulled the royal-blue bank sack out of her briefcase and laid it in front of him. 'Look.'

He picked it up and unzipped the top. The funky smell of cigarette smoke, marijuana, liquor and grease, ink and sweat, came out with the money. It was very dirty money, its filth redeemed entirely by the fact that there was such a lot of it.

'Oh, my Christ, you found more?' Delaney said, lining up the stacks in front of him. 'Where?' And then, because the money itself was more interesting than anything she could say about it, he lost interest in her answer. 'A lot of these are fifties, you know that? And hundreds. Wow. Lot of money.'

He looked up. Their faces blazed at him like two suns. He said, 'What?'

Sarah took two more bank sacks out of her briefcase and passed them across the desk. He unzipped them with his mouth open, too awestruck to say any more.

'I got my radio back, too,' Ray Menendez said.

SEVENTEEN

Robin drove south to Valencia and turned left, for no reason except it was a big, busy street with many cars. The next major stoplight was showing a green left-turn arrow as he approached it, so he turned left again into a residential neighborhood. When he saw an empty carport next to a house with the blinds closed, he pulled into it, turned off the motor and sat in shady silence, listening to the engine cool.

He knew the two detectives from the house had chased him – he'd seen the female running for her car. Probably they'd called for help. Nobody had been close enough to get his license number but they were good car-spotters so by now they'd have all the patrol cars in town looking for a white Taurus with new Michelins. They'd look in the streets, though, he reasoned – not in carports yet – and he needed a few minutes to decide on his next moves.

Nobody came out of the house to run him off so he sat in the vine-shaded space and sorted through his most urgent problems. This car, first. He had counted on having nine hours before the owner found it missing – plenty of time to get out of town. Now he needed to ditch it as soon as possible.

Or else . . . maybe he should run with it, right now. That could work – he was only a few blocks from the highway. He could be on I-19, headed for I-10 west, before they got everybody looking for him. And without a license number the highway patrol was not going to stop every white Taurus out there.

But he couldn't make LA on one tank of gas, and he wasn't carrying enough money to fill up again. He had a stolen credit card that he'd picked up in the Target checkout line while a distracted shopper argued with her child, but he'd had it since last week – it would almost certainly have been cancelled by now. He had a little money back in his pad on MacArthur

Street but the question was did the police have his identity yet? If they did they might have his address and they'd be watching for him now. If they could spare somebody for the job – he'd heard about all the budget cuts.

So many ifs. He had not worried about any of them before because he was sure he was going to have the money from the stash house . . . his brain hit a little glitch there, like a washboard road under tires. Those words, *the money from the stash house,* set off a firestorm of screaming rage in his mind, so hot he couldn't think.

That money, *shit shit shit!* was supposed to be his by now. He'd been thinking of it as his money, feeling a fierce joy of ownership about it for close to three months. He had planned it so carefully for so long, done all the smaller jobs – boosted a car, run a box of guns to the butt-puckery-dangerous rendezvous south of Sonoita – to keep himself in funds while he watched the house, planned the heist, assembled the weapons and crew. *And now it was gone in a blink? No! Shit shit shit!*

But he didn't have time now to let rage take over – he had to think! While he was still in Wilmot, Owen Chu had taught him some words that were supposed to calm you down, help you think under stress. He said they were called mantras.

'Isn't that what monks use?' Robin said. 'I thought you said you weren't a mystic.'

'I'm not,' Owen said. 'I just know some words that work if you say them over and over. Or sometimes just a sound will do it.'

Robin remembered one sound Owen recommended, and tried it now: 'Om om om.' He felt silly saying it so it didn't calm him down, and pretty soon it turned into, 'Om om om fucking shitface cops—' And then his gut was burning again. So he started over with the mantra he'd made up for himself, 'I am strong, I am great, I am golden, I will win.'

He said *that* ten times and was himself again: rational, cool. To test it, he let himself remember that first night, after he'd started watching the house with the heavy door, when he'd seen the black-haired man come out in the yard, take the cover off the jar that was buried out there, and add more money to the jar. And the feeling he got, right then, everything in him saying yes, I can do it. That money is *mine.*

His instincts had been right, though, that what he was seeing in the yard was just the skim; the main stash of money had to be in the house, where the people who set up this operation would have put it.

After he confirmed there was big money involved he had been totally systematic about making the heist work. Learned which days they made deliveries, which nights they got resupply. The money transfer took place every other Tuesday, he learned by careful watching. A man in a nice business suit came to the house, carrying a briefcase. It took a lot more watching and listening, and patience, patience, to figure out that the funny *clunk* he heard every time the suit man came was the table being tipped over. The second *clunk* and then a *scree-scree-scree* was the table being set back up and moved into place. When he was sure they were consistent he knew that the day to do it was the second Monday, the last day before the collector came again.

After that it was a matter of putting the crew together – three stupid guys who would be cannon fodder but not know it – and the just-crazy-enough plan to steal a service van at the last minute for cover. For the last month, all the time he wasn't watching the house he watched service vans around town, mapping their routes, where they were likely to be. And then, on that last day he'd found one he'd never watched! That was part of his method – you had to have a plan and then be willing to be flexible, make changes if something else worked better.

You couldn't be afraid to take chances. His mantras made him strong enough to take the last terrible chance, going in through the window with all the guns firing . . . walking right up to the back of the man firing an AK47 – how many guys could do that?

Now he had to do the next hard thing, which was kiss that money goodbye. He didn't want to believe it but he had to – the money was gone. Those two cops would go back there after they gave up on chasing him and figure out why he had the cover off the control box for the watering system, wouldn't they? He made himself say it out loud, softly, 'Yes, they would.' They would do that because that was what cops did – follow the evidence, figure out what was going on, decide what to do to get it stopped. Cops only ever had one basic thing they wanted – to get on top of the situation, whatever it was, and take control. Oh, yeah. Take control. Fucking shitface cops.

So he was not going to be the idiot who went back to make sure. He had escaped that bloody death house three days ago, survived those terrible nights in the parking garage. Escaped the damn place again today when he went for the money and those detectives were somehow right there where they had no business being. *How many times do I have to escape that one stupid house? Hell with it. Not the only money in the damn world. I'll get out of here and get some more.*

He had just over two hundred dollars in his squat on MacArthur in a bag that was packed, ready to go. The money was ridiculous compared to what he had expected to have when he left here, but it would get him to LA. There was no better answer to his problems. And his problems would get worse with every minute he hesitated. So he was going to go there right now and get that bag. *I am strong, I am great . . .* and I am in a white Taurus like a hundred others in this vicinity. He started the motor, backed out and headed for the Rodeo Grounds.

He'd been staying in a bed, bath and hotplate on MacArthur Street that he sometimes referred to, when he was far enough away from it, as 'my flat.' It was in a row of others just like it, in a converted ten-unit motel, squalid and scarred by generations of abuse. Old enough to have totally outmoded plumbing and light fixtures, it was on its second or third set of hollow-core doors. Nothing in the building was new, or was ever going to survive long enough to become antique.

Management always occupied the end unit, and changed every few months. The clientele was even more temporary – they left as soon as they could afford something better, or when they couldn't pay at all and got evicted.

Robin had lived there, off and on, since he got out of Wilmot prison. He moved out to live with women, moved back in when he tired of them. It suited him well enough – the management dealt in cash and did not ask for a deposit; it was cheap and the other tenants were so scruffy they made him feel successful. He was seldom home anyway, and always thought of himself as moving on, moving up, getting out of this dump any day. As soon as he made the big score, he had been telling himself.

Now he knew he had to go without his big score, just grab his bag and be gone. He had always hated losing and this loss was the bitterest since he got out of prison. His big chance to become a real player, and he had been working on it in secret so long – the disappointment burned in his gut. *I am strong, I am great . . .* He could handle it.

He had three or four favorite bars in the area – not to drink much, he was careful about that, but as adjunct living rooms. He cooled off or warmed up in them, met people and made deals. He lived by selling items for which there was no firm price, often to people with no fixed address. Their conversations were usually short, with an emphasis on body language, and ended when cash slid across the table to Robin. Robin never paid. Buying merchandise was for chumps, he believed. He stole to restock.

The sports bar called Ricky's was one of his favorite spots. Designed for noise addicts who liked their decibel levels just below nosebleed, it was dark and featured six big television screens showing professional sports. The babble from all those games was so noisy that no conversation was audible for more than two feet. In case it ever was, the place had small round tables and wooden chairs with metal glides that screeched when they were dragged across the bare tile floor, which they frequently were by groups of happy men who clustered in front of the screens and screamed orders for more beer. At Ricky's you could sell crack, fence a firearm, or agree to an assault, make the deal and collect the cash in peace and safety because the people at the next table would not have heard a word you said.

After he backed out of the carport off Valencia Road, he drove to his neighborhood where he circled the block around his building twice, looking for trouble. The two cars in the lot in front of his building belonged to tenants. There were no black-and-whites circling, or unmarked Crown Vics with plainclothes detectives sitting in them, pretending to read newspapers. It looked OK to go in. He decided to drive on to Ricky's, park this Taurus in Ricky's lot and walk back cautiously, looking all around. If all went well he would retrieve his bag from his flat, come back to the Taurus and drive out of town, fast.

It was just past noon, so Ricky's lot was about half full. The place served burgers and a few other sandwiches to attract people who liked to booze at lunchtime. A couple of cars he recognized – the liquor salesman's Nissan, the roofing guys' pickup – they were here almost every day. And there was the beat-up blue Saturn full of books and trash, belonging to that ditsy college girl he called, in his mind, the Snotty Student. Came down from the campus with her boyfriends, swinging that long hair around, looking to score some crack. Robin had never sold to her and didn't intend to, didn't need her kind of trouble.

He parked as far away from the street as he could, around the corner in one of the three overflow spots on the side of the building. Quick, while there was nobody around to see, he unzipped his pants, slid the Derringer out of the little holster he had sewn in his crotch and buttoned it into his right-hand cargo pocket. Since he had spun the ignition on this car and had no key, he couldn't lock the steering gear or the doors. He turned the motor off with his short-handled screwdriver, put the tool in his left-hand pocket and walked back to his place.

He walked straight to his door, not letting himself look around. He put the key in the lock and slipped inside without looking back. Leaned against the door with his heart beating fast, ka-bam, ka-bam. *So far so good. Hey, I can change into a shirt that fits.*

He opened his bag, found a plain white T-shirt and changed into it. The stolen shirt from the hospital, *what shall I . . .* Thinking it might furnish some kind of a trail, he rolled it up tight, put the roll by the door so he wouldn't forget it. His money was where he'd left it, in the zippered inside pocket of the bag, alongside two joints and a dime bag of crack. He took two twenties from the money clip and put the rest back, used the toilet, washed his hands and face. *OK, no more stalling, here we go.*

Still no extra cars in the lot. He passed a Dumpster and dropped the shirt inside.

Two blocks to Ricky's. *That little doctor won't be getting off shift for hours yet. This is going to be just fine. One block more – God, it's hot.*

The parking lot looked the same as before. The front door of Ricky's opened as he walked past, letting out an inviting blast of cold air. *Maybe I should get some water . . . no, forget it. Keep going.* He walked straight and firm past the door of Ricky's Sports Bar and around the corner to where his car . . . *Oh, shit.*

A black-and-white patrol car was drawn up behind the Taurus, which abruptly was not his car any more. Now it belonged once again to the female physician with a cute butt who worked at Children's Hospital and must have come out mid-shift and found it gone. The driver's-side door was open now, the cap was off the ignition, and the patrol officer who had inspected its butchered disks was on his radio, calling in the license number.

Robin turned smoothly and headed back to Ricky's door. Another patrol car was just pulling into the lot, parking along-side the first. Robin walked into the dark, cool bar, where the insane noise level hit him like a fist. Hoping his bag was not too conspicuous, he walked toward the men's room. Halfway across the room, he saw the long-haired girl, the Snotty Student. She was sitting alone in a booth, nursing the last inch of a beer and scanning the room with her do-me eyes. She even had a couple of textbooks on the table, like she might be going to study any minute. What a laugh.

His stomach turned acid at the thought of dealing with her anxiety and her lacerating tongue. But he told himself, *She's got a car and she's here for the old wants and needs. My kind of a girl.*

To get his mojo working, he took a deep renewing breath and held it, the way Owen Chu had taught him. As he let it out he said fiercely in the deepest part of his brain, *Fair game, fair game.* He walked quietly to where she sat facing away from him and bent till his lips were next to her ear. That way he didn't have to shout when he said, 'Every time I see you in here I want to tell you how beautiful your hair is.'

She turned the full force of her bright eyes on him and said, without smiling, 'That's pretty lame but it'll work if you buy me a beer.' Robin slid his bag into the seat across from her and waved to the waitress, who was already watching them. In two minutes they each had a beer and he was learning that her name was Valerie.

'Mine's Richard,' he said, and then, watching her eyes, 'but you can call me Dick if you feel like it.'

'We'll see,' she said. 'What about the nuts?' He blinked and she laughed, pointing to the sacks of mixed nuts that hung on a rack behind the bar. He got the waitress back and ordered a sack for each of them.

'Bring some of those eggs, too,' she said, pointing to the jar of hard-boiled eggs, disgusting, he thought, on the end of the bar. 'And a bowl of popcorn, will you?' She nodded at him as if confirming something he'd said, though he hadn't said anything. It was kind of fascinating, watching her wants and needs keep bubbling up. 'Salty stuff goes good with the beer, hmmm?'

'I like more salt with my salty stuff,' Robin said, and shook some over the eggs from the shaker on the table. He shook some over his hand too, and then over hers, and they both licked their hands, watching each other do it. Her laugh was like worn gears shifting, metal on metal.

The two patrolmen walked in and stood by the bar, chatting with the bartender. Robin dredged up some more jokes, making sure Tucson's finest would see two young students, laughing and flirting in a booth. Valerie was helping him, pretending she found everything he said very funny. Her eyes were a raptor's eyes now; she was on the hunt. Robin pushed his bag aside and slid around the booth to sit beside her.

'This way I don't have to yell,' he said.

'And if things get slow we can lick each other's hands,' she said, and they laughed together.

When their beer was a little over half gone, he stretched

lazily, sighed, and said drinking beer always made him want to smoke a joint.

She stretched in imitation of him and said, a little too loud, 'Oh, Lordy, that sounds like a grand plan!'

'OK,' Robin said, as softly as possible, into her ear. 'But let's not share that idea with our friends who are just leaving,' nodding at the two officers who had handed their cards to the bartender and were going back out to their cars, 'because all those legal marijuana plans don't seem to have quite gelled yet.'

'Oh, right,' she said, quiet at once, desperate to keep him thinking about the plan, 'souls of discretion here.'

'Absolutely. So here's how I think we ought to do this,' he said. Conspiratorial, enlisting her help. She was giddy with anticipation so she never questioned his statement that he didn't have the weed on him and had to go get it. 'But I don't want to get you involved in that part, so after we finish this beer and I go to the men's room,' he was making it up as he went along, 'give me a couple of minutes,' pulling ideas out of the air, 'and then take your books on out to your car . . .'

She was nodding, nodding. Anything, her face said, just bring me the dope.

She agreed to meet him on a corner a couple of blocks north. Robin used the men's room, came out and turned right instead of left – the back door was just a step away.

EIGHTEEN

Doris' neighbor was named Betty Lou, 'Like half the other girls in my high school class,' she said. 'For a while there after I got married I thought about changing it to something exotic like Hedy or Rosalind, but my husband said, "Oh, honey, can't you let it be?"' She sighed. 'I was kind of an adventurer at heart but Clem was never much for trying new things.'

Before he'd finished fixing the venetian blind over her sink, Zeb knew a lot more than that about Clem – his widow had shared details of his digestion, TV viewing habits and problems with footwear. Zeb got the new cord threaded through the holes in the blind all right but he was desperately afraid that before he got the spider gear to work she would have progressed to Clem's sexual proclivities, and he would have to plead a sick headache and leave without his haircut.

But he got the stupid thing turning just in time, and they had so much fun crowing about his success that she forgot about Clem and got absorbed in details of Zeb's haircut. He had come over to her house determined to get a super-short one, high and tight like a marine so it would last. But Betty Lou talked him out of it.

'Honey,' she said, turning him in the rotating chair she kept in her front bay window, 'you've got just the right head and that nice thick hair for the Justin Bieber 'do, why in the world would you want to change it?'

'Well, it grows out so fast—'

'So what? I'm right here, and I've got so many repair jobs— Shucks, Zeb, you could get free haircuts for months just fixing the doorknobs and dresser drawers in this place.' Those all sounded like jobs he could do, but how much more would he have to know about Clem before they were done?

When she got out her beautician's tools, though, the change was amazing, she became Betty Lou the proud artiste. No more stories while *she* was working. She snipped away at him for half an hour and followed the cut with a blow-dry and brush-out, humming to herself. Finally she handed him the mirror, twirled him around so he could see the back in the panel mirror by the window and said, 'How about *that*?' making it clear she expected praise.

And he had to admit, it looked just as good as the first time in the Unisex shop, maybe a tad better. So he said it was fine, thanks.

'No need to thank me, this is strictly business,' she said. 'Why don't you come back next week and oil my hinges? I'll give you a manicure and pedicure that'll make you feel like King Hussein of Jordan. Clem used to say that when I fixed his feet he felt like it would be just a shame to walk on them ever again.' She laughed heartily at that old chestnut and Zeb did his best to join in.

By then he was beginning to think of his haircut as well earned, so he said he'd let her know after he found out how much work Doris had lined up for him. Walking home he decided that if he had to adopt somebody to survive, it was a lucky chance he'd found Doris at that bus stop. She might be a tough old bird and critical about a lot of things but at least she didn't have a jolly little story about every item in her damn life.

'Looks like that deal worked out OK,' Doris said when he got home. 'You and Betty Lou get along all right?'

'Fine,' he said. 'She's quite a talker, though, isn't she?'

Looking oddly pleased, Doris said, 'How about a quick run to Walmart before lunch? Then we need to move some boxes into the shed this afternoon and get groceries, but maybe if we do all that fast we could read another couple of chapters before dinner, what do you think?'

NINETEEN

'Turns out buried treasure's no fun even after you get it back to the station,' Sarah said. 'Did you ever think you could get so sick of counting money?'

'And signing my name,' Ray said. 'A few days ago I couldn't even spell affidavit; this week I've signed so many my hand hurts.'

'Too bad we didn't have the cut-out money yesterday when we did that dog-and-pony for the media. You think the chief will make us do another one?'

Ray's grin was a dazzling flash of white teeth in his brown face. 'Might be worth it to see Delaney making cute again with the TV reporters.'

'You ever see him smile like that before?'

'Never. I have to say, Sarah, I think you furnished a little too much contrast. Standing there with your "let's wait till we catch the ex-dead-guy" face on, really . . .'

'Bite your tongue. That was my "I just came back from three autopsies" face.'

'Oh, that's right, your feet hurt. Anyway, now we got all this money, this is the time when all the agencies work together and we tighten the net – isn't that the plan?'

'You sound dubious.'

'Dubious doesn't begin to cover it,' Ray said. 'Any plan that includes catching Robin the ex-dead-guy gets a big laugh from me.'

'Why can't we catch that little sneak? Are you going to nose around for his address by the rodeo grounds some more? Check your snitches, ask if anybody's seen him?'

'You bet. Right now. You?'

'Delaney says ballistics found something – says come to his office in ten.'

'Say you couldn't find me, OK? I've got a . . .' he made a mock-swaggering move with his shoulders, 'a *hunch*.'

'Wow. Just like in the movies. OK, you better go on while I still can't see you.'

Delaney's office was too small to hold all his detectives sitting down, so discussions in his office were more like a bivuac than a meeting. Jason perched on the console and Oscar leaned against the file cabinet.

'Banjo found a match between the guns we turned in and a recent heist. Ah, good, here he is now.' Delaney got everybody to move a couple of inches so they could wedge in one more chair.

Banjo Bailey, the crime lab's chemist and firearms expert, got his nickname moonlighting with a bluegrass band. He looked like a benign pixie with complex hair; he had a mustache whose upswept waxed ends were art works and a long pigtail at the back. Curled up on the chair nearest the door, he peered at them over his little round wire-frames and said, 'This is a rare thing – looks like we might be going to solve a recent burglary case while we investigate this homicide. I entered the serial number on one of your guns and pulled up a list that matched almost everything you turned in.'

'Way to go,' Ollie said.

'Yeah. It's an odd list, too. Couple of quite valuable weapons, and the rest range from average to nearly worthless. But all taken in one break-in back in March.'

Delaney said, 'Let's see, Ollie, did you send me that list we talked about? Ah, yes, here it is.' He brought up his list, and soon all the detectives were standing around his computer screen or Banjo's laptop.

'Start with the Glock .45,' Delaney said, and read off a serial number.

'Yeah. I got it,' Banjo said. 'Let me read it back to you,' and read the same number off his list.

Delaney said, 'How about a Smith & Wesson revolver?' He read a serial number. Banjo echoed it off his list. 'OK, that's the two men in the yard,' Ollie said.

'Now . . . you didn't turn in a .22 caliber weapon from that crime scene,' Banjo said, 'but Sarah brought me a .22 slug out of one of her autopsies this week, and I think I've got the weapon that fired it on my list here.'

'You have?' Delaney was looking at him like a kid who's just spotted an ice-cream truck.

'Yup. I'm about eighty-five percent certain that slug was fired by a Derringer .22 caliber two-shot.' He read off a number.

'Well, we won't have a serial number till we catch the guy who's carrying it,' Delaney said. 'But we think that gun belongs to the bad guy who's still out there.'

'The one the papers call "the lone survivor?"'

'We've been calling him the ex-dead-guy,' Sarah said. 'But now it's pretty certain his name is Robin Brady.'

'And it figures that he provided the guns for this attack, doesn't it?' Delaney said. 'Theft is his favorite crime – burglary, break-ins. That's what he went to prison for. This stash house is his first armed invasion – that we know of, anyway. He's moving up, the way they do.'

'But why in the world,' Banjo said, 'would anybody carry a little trinket like that Derringer to invade a stash house?'

'Because it's so good for concealed carry,' Jason said. 'Robin likes to carry his firepower in his undies.'

'My stars,' Banjo said.

Jason muttered, 'Country to the bone.'

'I brought one to show you.' It nested easily in Banjo's slender palm. The handle was ivory, yellowed with age. 'Two barrels, see? They swing to the side like this to reload. Small weapon, but high velocity – used at close range it can be lethal.'

'Eighty-five percent,' Sarah said. 'Can we take that to court and win with it?'

'Guess you'd have to if you were going to trial today,' Banjo said, serenely smiling, 'because it's the best I can do with what I've got now. The bullet was badly damaged by bouncing around the inside of a skull. But of course after you capture the suspect, I can test-fire his weapon, put some pictures on a projector, show some lands and grooves that match, and have a jury well persuaded . . .' He crossed his legs and cleared his throat. 'When and if you can *catch* the guy.' He peered around the room humorously. 'And if he's obliging enough to still be carrying the same gun . . .' All the detectives looked at their notes in silence. Finally Banjo turned a page and asked them, 'What about the Desert Eagle?'

Ollie raised his eyebrows. 'You mean you've got one of those on your list too?'

'Sure do. Have you?'

'Well, yes, but . . . it can't be a match to yours.'

'You sure?' He read off a serial number.

Ollie blinked and said, 'Say it again.' Sarah watched Ollie as Banjo read it again. His face remained stoical but his ears twitched just before he said, 'It matches. How can that be?' He looked at Delaney as if he was owed an explanation.

'I have no idea,' Delaney said.

Banjo said, 'What's the problem?'

'The Desert Eagle,' Sarah said, 'we all thought until right now was being fired by one of the guards in the stash house.'

'All right,' Banjo said politely. He looked around the room, puzzled to see so many detectives who seemed to think he was raining on their parade. 'I still don't see—'

'Up until now this conversation was proving that Robin Brady stole those guns. Agreed, guys?' Everybody nodded. 'Which works with our growing perception, mine anyway, that Robin Brady was the leader of this gang that invaded the stash house.'

'I think so, too,' Ollie said, and Oscar and Jason said together, 'Me, too.'

'Well, but, he couldn't have stolen all the guns on *both* sides. Could he?'

'Ray keeps saying he's hot,' Ollie said, 'but I can't see any way that would work.'

Sarah leaned toward Ellsworth's elaborately groomed face and asked him softly, 'You don't have a Kalashnikov on that list, do you?'

'Um . . . no.'

'Ah.' She sat back, not knowing whether to feel relieved or more puzzled.

'I do have a Lorcin .25 caliber semi-auto,' Ellsworth said. 'Anybody interested in that?'

Ollie said, 'No.'

'Don't blame you,' Banjo said. 'Lame excuse for a weapon.'

'I've heard that,' Jason said. 'You ever fired one?'

'In the lab,' Banjo said. 'Which is the only place I would fire one. It's got a nasty habit of jamming every few rounds.'

'But we don't have one so why are we talking about it?' Delaney said. 'Any other guns on that list, Banjo?'

'No.'

'Then let's get back to the Desert Eagle.'

'Wait,' Sarah said. 'Can we back up to the Lorcin a minute?'

Delaney frowned. 'Why?'

'Remember the video of the running man? He had a small handgun tucked in his waistband. Can't we blow up some stills of that shot and show them to Banjo?' she asked the criminalist. 'You'd know one if you saw it, wouldn't you?'

'Sure, if you've got a pretty good view of most of it.'

'I think we do. It would settle the question we've never answered, boss,' Sarah said. 'Whether the running man had any connection to this crime?'

'OK,' Delaney said. 'Do it. Now . . . the Desert Eagle. If it's on both lists it must have been stolen at the same time as the other three guns, right?' He looked at all the nodding heads. 'By the same person, don't you suppose?'

'We don't know he was alone,' Oscar said.

'Good point,' Delaney said. 'Banjo, do you know if they lifted any prints at that job?'

'I heard not. Techies said they dusted and dusted, didn't get squat.'

'Robin likes to wear gloves,' Sarah said.

'No offense,' Oscar said, 'but is it possible, Ollie, you got one number wrong?'

Ollie shook his head. 'I went over this list several times – last of all with Stan from the evidence room. He read it back like you're doing now. So there's no way—' He met Delaney's eyes boring into him and sighed. 'But I'll go back to the evidence room and check my list one more time against the gun.'

'And when you prove you didn't make a mistake,' Sarah said, remembering the table in the stash house with all the guns and ammo lined up in careful rows, 'what other scenarios will be left to consider?'

'It wasn't old Baldy's gun after all,' Jason said.

'In that case what was he firing? It was the only gun near him.'

'Robin had a partner in the burglary,' Oscar suggested, 'who also likes to wear gloves. And sell what he steals.'

'Or Robin was alone at the burglary,' Jason said, 'and running a little short of cash . . .' He loved speculation, called it 'story time.' 'So he decided to sell the biggest, most badass gun of the lot—'

'I would have thought that would be the Dirty Harry,' Sarah said.

'Ah, here we go with old Clint Eastwood again,' Banjo clucked, disparaging. 'Cowboy actor boosts his asking price by showing he can hold a .44 Magnum steady with one hand.'

'I've always figured he had a light plastic replica,' Jason said.

'Shame on you,' Ollie said. 'Clint wouldn't cheat.'

'Made the gun's fortune, too,' Banjo said. 'It's been the famous "Dirty Harry" ever since. Many a macho American male's walking around with a messed-up rotator cuff from trying to shoot the .44 Magnum the way Clint did it in the movies.'

Sarah said, 'It's too heavy for me even with two hands.'

'You've tried it? I'm surprised.'

She shrugged. 'Somebody was always urging me to, so finally I did.'

'And?'

'I completely destroyed a target and both arms hurt for two days.'

'Well, so think about it – Robin and his mark are talking high-powered weapons,' Jason said, getting back into the story. 'Robin offers the S&W but the guy for some reason wants the Eagle instead.' He was really grooving on his narrative now, patting his head and bouncing one knee. 'Said, "Nah, I like the one with the big brass slide." '

'I could see it happening that way,' Banjo said. 'Some bad guys think they have to impress with their armament. Haven't you noticed that? Like, a guy who likes to carry a knife will usually carry two knives.'

'Try to get done up like a real mad dog,' Jason said. 'Yeah.'

'And for a guy like that who's trying to bootstrap up from

bad guy to terrifying guy, he sees that Desert Eagle pistol, it weighs over four pounds and looks like it's built to fight a war—'

'Which I think it was, originally,' Ollie said. 'Designed for the Israeli Army, right?'

'Yes. Made here now, though,' Banjo said.

Ollie said, 'I tried one once, at the range.'

'And?'

'If I was an Israeli boy and they told me I had to shoot that thing every week, I would think about joining the Palestinians.'

'It kicks that bad?'

'Like a mule.'

'But some persons with felonious intent regard that as a personal challenge,' Jason said. 'So Old Baldy loves the way the Desert Eagle keeps trying to break both his wrists! Says, "Hey, bitchin', I'll take it, how much?" '

'And Robin's buyer just happens to be one of the guys guarding the stash house?' Delaney shook his head. 'That's way too much coincidence for me.'

'Yes.' Sarah lit up, suddenly, thinking. 'But if you turn it around . . . suppose Robin decided he could spare one gun and went looking for a buyer. He finds a guy who says he wants something that shoots serious ammo. They talk about the awesome power of the seven rounds of .50 AE the Eagle will carry, and Robin makes the sale. By the time they're done talking he decides Baldy must be into something interesting and follows him home. As soon as he sees the heavy metal door with two locks . . .'

'Now *that* sounds just like our Robin,' Jason said, 'doesn't it? Sooo clever. I can just see him lurking around that house – he'd cuddle a cactus if he had to.'

'Yeah,' Ollie said. 'Tricky ol' Robin motoring around that Midvale Park neighborhood in two or three different vehicles, hiding in the bushes? Watching them move the coke and weed till he figured it all out.'

Banjo said, 'You guys kind of love this crazy hoodlum, don't you?'

'He's interesting to watch,' Sarah said. 'He'll be more fun to catch.'

'Man,' Ray said, walking in, 'I hate to tell you this . . .'

'Then don't,' Delaney said. 'Where have you been?'

'Down near the Rodeo Grounds, nosing around, showing Robin's picture to people . . . and I think we just missed ol' Robin again.'

The whole table said, 'What?'

Delaney said, 'Missed him where?'

'I told you, near the Rodeo Grounds. I heard chatter on my radio – Norm Sapperstein talking about a white Taurus with Michelin tires. He was over on Twelfth Street at Ricky's Bar. Said he heard that Need To Locate we put out, so when he saw the rear end of a white Taurus poking out from the side of Ricky's he drove in to have a look. It was unlocked and the ignition was spun, so he called it in and he was standing by it, waiting for a tow, when I found him.'

Sarah said, 'How'd you know it's the Taurus we chased?'

'I didn't. But I went in and showed the bartender Robin's picture and he said, "Hell, that guy just left here." I asked if he was alone and he said, 'He was when he came in, but he hooked up with that long-haired girl from the university, she's here a lot.'

'I can't stand it,' Sarah said. 'How can we keep running into him like this and yet he stays one step ahead?'

'I told you, the guy is hot. He may not be with the girl any more, either. I went back out and told Sapperstein, and he said, 'You know, that's funny. I noticed them in the bar. I thought they were getting it on but she came out alone and drove away.'

'In what?' Delaney said.

'An old blue Saturn. Very dirty, Norm said, and the whole back seat full of trash. Books and papers, piles of stuff in there – she's a real slob.'

'Oh. But he didn't get the license number?'

'No. He wasn't interested in her at the time.'

'What about Robin?' Ollie asked him. 'Did Sapperstein see him leave?'

'No. He said, "I've been right here, waiting for the tow. I'd have seen him if he came out this way." So I went back again and asked the barkeep. He said, "I never saw him leave, but I been busy. Maybe he went out the back."'

'Out the back,' Sarah said. 'That sounds like Robin.'

'Out the back, one step ahead,' Ray said. 'I love this little turd.'

'Sarah,' Phyllis from cold cases said, sticking her head in, 'your desk phone's been ringing and ringing, so I answered it and a girl on there says she has to talk to you personally.'

Sarah ran toward the phone, thinking, *Denny!*

A voice said, 'I still don't want to get involved.'

'OK. I'll keep you out of it,' Sarah said. 'Who is this?'

'Janet Butts, of course,' she said. 'Who else would it be? Jeez.'

Sarah stifled an impulse to estimate how many other people it might have been. 'You think of something to tell me?'

'I just saw Zeb again in that same car. It's the weirdest thing. He was with this old lady.'

'Oh? Which old lady?'

'Nobody *I* ever saw before, for sure. He was driving, but it looked like she was telling him where to go.'

'Where'd you see them, Janet?'

'At the Walmart's on Valencia – I was turning in and they were pulling out.'

'A gray Buick, you said?'

'Yes.'

'Anything else you can tell me? Like, did you notice any numbers on the license plate?'

'Well, sure, I got it all – why else would I be calling you?'

Too pleased with the information to brood about how annoying the messenger was, Sarah wrote it down. 'I certainly do thank you for this,' she said, and promised again that Zeb would never hear from her that his sister had . . . she couldn't say 'narced on him,' although in her family they'd have called it that. She said, 'been involved,' and hung up quickly.

She pulled up the DMV database and entered the number. In a few seconds the registration appeared on the screen. The car was a late-nineties Buick LeSabre belonging to Mrs Doris Duncan at an address on Camino de la Tierra. There was no lienholder listed; Doris' car was paid for.

Sarah copied the information and trotted back to Delaney's desk, crying out to a roomful of detectives who seemed to be too busy to listen, 'Wouldn't it be handy if guns carried all their information with them the way cars do?'

'We don't have time for any of your rants right now,' Delaney said. 'Everybody's going to Ricky's Bar. Come on, you can ride with Jason.'

'Not me,' Sarah said. 'That's what I'm trying to tell you. I just found out where Zeb is.'

It took two minutes of very fast talk to convince him. The other detectives were all loading up, talking to the SWAT team Delaney had requested to go with them.

'If you all get down there right away,' Delaney said, 'you can get enough information from the people in that bar – this is our chance to catch that dirty bugger.'

'If I find Zeb,' Sarah said, 'I'll find Robin.'

'You don't know that for sure,' Delaney said.

'I know they're friends,' Sarah said. 'His mother said so. And I know Zeb's been driving this woman's car. It's the best break we've had.'

'Well, I'm not letting you go alone,' Delaney said. 'Jason, you go with her.'

'OK if I drive?' Jason said, as they put on their weapons, found their vests. 'No offense,' he said as she fixed him with a stony stare. 'I just like to drive.'

TWENTY

The plan worked just the way Robin had designed it in that dizzy improvisation in the bar. He walked quickly away from the back door and down the alley, wishing he could see what those cops were doing out front. What would they think when Valerie came out by herself? He'd done everything but hang a sign over the booth saying, 'This is how you do seduction.'

Valerie was waiting at the corner they'd agreed on. After they threw a lot of books and trash into the back so he could get into the passenger seat of her spectacularly messy car, she suggested they go to Rudy Garcia Park, saying she thought of it as her own private green space.

Robin didn't tell her how many deals he had made there – after bars, parks were his favorite workspace. He was considering her car – it would be humiliating to leave Tucson in this terrible old clunker, but on the other hand, maybe it was good cover? Anyway, it would get him on the road. The surprise at the stash house had pretty much cancelled his determination to off Zeb before he left town – his need to get out of town took precedence over everything else now.

While he was still deciding whether it would be beneath him to take Valerie's car, as they approached a gas station she said, 'Oh, Richard, could you be a pal and loan me some gas money? Otherwise we might not make it to the park. I just noticed I'm on empty.'

'Why, so you are.' He saw that the needle was sitting right on 'E.' 'You always run around town on the fumes?'

'Well, I don't believe in babying these cars,' she said, snickering, tossing her long hair around as she parked by the pump. 'They need to be told who's boss.' Probably spent her last cash in the bar. Crazy broad.

Although not too crazy, come to think of it, to maneuver

him into getting out and filling her gas tank, and watching contentedly while he paid for it.

And fully alert, really at the top of her game, when it came time to enjoy a fat joint in the park. She drove around for a while, looking critical, saying, 'Let's find a nice quiet parking place in the shade.' There were plenty of shady places inside the park, but she didn't want to go in there and 'squat on the grass with the bums,' she wanted to stay in the car. It didn't seem to occur to her that her car was the most squalid spot in the neighborhood – maybe in the whole city.

She finally settled on a spot under a tall cypress, pulled her car up tight against the curb to get it all in the shade and rolled down the windows. She got very happy when they lit up, waved her hands extravagantly at the park as if showing off her private estate and said, 'Isn't this *heaven*?'

Rudy Garcia Park was not at all heavenly, but kind of nice in its own way, Robin thought – a worn, homey place with tired grass and some beat-up playground equipment, a few benches and a baseball field. It certainly wasn't private – it got plenty of use, Robin knew, by big local families and the people who brought their horses to the Rodeo Grounds next door. Valerie probably liked it because nobody bothered her when she came here to get high. The people in this part of town usually had too many problems of their own to give a damn what anybody else was doing.

Robin pretended to join her but didn't actually smoke much. There was a lot to decide yet and he needed his head clear. He was still a little in shock from finding that cop back there by the Taurus – he'd had to make so many changes, so fast. A planner by nature, he kept thinking, did I leave any loose ends? Other than Zeb he couldn't think of any, but the uncertainty made him inclined to settle for this car – too much had gone wrong; he needed to get out of Tucson and cool off for a while. Valerie's old crate ought to get him as far as Yuma and he could switch to a better car there.

After a little more of this happy smoke she would be too dizzy to drive. He would get her to give him the keys. There'd be no screaming in a public park, no mess to clean up. He could drive them both out of here smiling and once he was on the road just throw her out anywhere. It was the sensible thing to do, he decided.

As soon as he made up his mind he was impatient to go, so when her eyes started to glaze a little he said, 'I think I've got a pipe in my bag. How would you like to drop a little crack into that weed and have a bit of a blast?'

'Oh, baby,' she said, her head on one side, beaming at him, 'does a polar bear poop on the ice?'

She had little gold scissors in her surprisingly neat make-up bag. She used it to cut what she called 'the burn-y part' off the joint, along with another half inch of weed, and drop it in the bowl of his 'sweet little tiger-striped pipe.' While he was clipping off a pebble of crack she wrapped the rest of the marijuana neatly in half a Kleenex and tucked it tenderly in her glove compartment. Against the backdrop of the sordid mess she had made of her car, her meticulous moves with the remains of the toke were enchanting to watch. Robin also noted how smoothly she had assumed ownership of the rest of the joint. This girl has all the right instincts, he thought. If only she had fewer needs I'd consider making her a partner.

As it was, if he took her car he would have to dispose of her. I'll wait till I'm clear out of town, he decided, past Marana, into that empty stretch between Red Rock and Picacho. Just push her out – she's a girl, stoned or not she's got round legs and all that hair; someone will pick her up. She might report the car stolen, but he'd have left it behind long before anybody got around to looking for it.

She got manic for a few minutes on the fresh smoke, talked a blue streak and giggled a lot. Then the chemical warfare began, between the mellowing Mary Jane and the speed-up effect of the crack. Her brain was trying to follow two different emotional tracks and the confusion made her angry. Resentment came pouring out of her, about school for the stupid courses that never translate to anything useful in the real world, then aimed at her parents for being so careless about their mutual cheating that they ended up divorced.

'Really,' she said, 'wouldn't you think they could have the

decency to sneak around?' But no, they'd split the sheets and left her stranded in student housing with nobody around to give a damn about her but her grandmother, and now even Gram was getting freaky.

Robin thought he must have heard wrong the first time she said that – he would never have guessed this girl to have family issues; she seemed like somebody raised under a rock. But no, there it was again, coming through the cloud of smoke, 'some fond granny *she* turns out to be. All those digs at me about sitting in bars when I should be studying – now some weirdo carries her groceries and she thinks tats and an eyebrow ring are just fine.'

Robin said, 'Why do you care if your granny has a boyfriend?' Just passing the time. She wasn't quite at the tipping point yet – might as well talk.

'Omigod, he's not her boyfriend, puh-*leese*!' Hair flying around, smoke billowing. 'I mean, he's not much older that I am. She may have her quirks but my grandmother is not depraved.'

'Nothing like her granddaughter, hmm?'

'Oh, good one. You think crack's so depraved you keep a supply on hand, right?' You couldn't insult her – she just batted them back. Another puff and then anger boiling up again. 'Silly little sneak fixed her car!'

He was absolutely not interested – but a stoner girl who seemed to think auto repair was a criminal offense, you had to ask – 'That makes you mad?'

'It's been up on blocks for weeks! Just because I had that little problem and blew a tire when I backed over the . . . never mind. She was pissed because I took it without asking her while she was at her neighbor's playing that stupid game with the tiles.'

'Scrabble?'

'No, not that, the Chinese one old women play, Ma somebody.'

'Never heard of it. I still don't get why you're mad.'

'She made me think it was wrecked beyond repair, some-thing wrong with the motor, too. Now Mr Eyebrow-ring's driving her around in it and when I ask her does she need me

to come over and read to her she says, "Never mind, honey,
I know you're busy and Zeb can read well enough."'

Robin sat up. 'His name is Zeb? As in Zebulon?'

'I don't know as in what. Why do you care?'

'I don't. I used to know a guy by that name, that's all. He
has an eyebrow ring?'

'Yes. And too many colorful tattoos to count. And now my
supposedly conservative grandmother, who until last week
depended on me for everything, driving and reading and
keeping her in touch with my father, who's flying around the
world all distraught because my mother is the worst wife and
mother in the world, an all-around flop as a human being . . .'
She disappeared into the smoke for a few seconds, came out
and said, 'Where was I?'

'You were telling me how you drive your Granny around.
Why? Did she lose her license?'

'Yes. She has macular . . . something. Blind spots.'

'But she kept her car? What kind of a car is it?'

'Umm . . . Buick.' Valerie's eyes had begun to blur. 'Nice
gray Buick LeSabre with clean upholstery. Oh, and one like-
new tire.' She giggled.

'Why'd you take it? Is it newer than your car?'

'Not newer but in better shape, and always full of gas.' She
turned her smoldering gaze on him, attentive suddenly. 'Why?
You thinking of stealing it?'

'Of course not,' said Robin, who of course was. 'How could
you take it without her knowing? Didn't you have to get the
keys?'

'I've got my own.' She tossed the hair around some more.
'Back when she trusted me for everything, she had a set made.'

'Didn't she make you give them back after you messed up
the tire?'

'She tried.' Valerie disappeared into the smoke for a few
seconds, came out coughing. When she could breathe again,
she told him, 'I told her I'd lost them but I'd keep looking. I
thought, why give them back? She'll get it fixed and I'll get
back on her good side. But then she started saying there was
something else wrong with the car, she might never be able
to fix it.'

'Older people can be so selfish, can't they? If she can't drive it she should let you have it.'

'We were kind of edging up to that deal when I . . . blew it. Blew the tire, blew the deal. And now that she's picked up stupid Zeb with the eyebrow ring, looks like she doesn't need her one and only granddaughter any . . . mmm.' She sucked hard several times, took the pipe out of her mouth and stared at it. 'Whass matter with this pipe?'

'Looks like it's empty. You mean your granny just found this person named Zeb? He just started helping her this week?'

'Yes. He turned up at the bus stop Tuesday morning and carried her grocery bags home. So now he's her hero. They're fixing everything in her house and the last I heard he was starting on the neighbors.'

It can't be, Robin thought, but . . . the eyebrow ring and the tats . . . It wasn't possible he could have enough luck to find Zeb and a better car just by accident like this, but what if . . .? *It's too fantastic.* But it would be dumb to be this close and not find out. He looked at his watch, pretending to think about the time. 'You know, I really have to go.'

'Aw, come on, I'm just getting comfy.' She slid a fingertip slowly up his arm, along his collarbone and up his neck to his mouth. ''S'nice here in the shade. Let's light up another jolt and get better acquainted.' He sat watching her, getting impatient. *She should be limp by now. God, she's just one big appetite.*

'It's great, but I have to get going,' he said, keeping it amiable. 'But listen, I'll make you a deal. You're a little too lit up to drive anyway, so why don't you move over here,' he opened his door, 'and I'll come around and put a little more crack in that pipe. You can have fun while I drive you to your grandmother's house.' He was out, closing the door, walking around.

'Oh, for God's sake,' she said when he opened her door, 'why would we want to go *there*?'

'Because if it turns out this Zeb character is the one I know, I have a little business to talk over with him.'

She tossed her hair back, sighed. He could see she knew, in the part of her head that was still tracking a little, that going to Granny's house was the oddest idea she had ever heard from a date. She was basically shrewd, too, so she must realize there was something damned odd about her new friend's interest in her grandmother's car. But he had said the magic word, 'crack,' and the drugs owned her now, so she moved.

The keys were still in the ignition. He fixed the smoke first, held the lighter for her, got it going. She had trouble dredging up the name of the street, but she told him to head out Valencia and it would come to her. She never did get it all right, but as they approached the bus stop corner she recognized it and told him to turn right. She was slurring her words badly by then, and when they reached the unmanned gate on Camino de la Tierra, she just tapped his arm, said, 'Mmm-mm,' and pointed inside.

Robin drove through the gate, past the empty caretaker's booth. He was taking it slow, letting Valerie point and murmur her way toward Grandmother's house. They rounded a little curve and then another, and there, just ahead, was a pink house with a gray Buick in its carport. An older model, true, but clean and well kept, looking like a trouble-free ride to Yuma and perhaps beyond.

And none other than his old friend Zebulon was unloading groceries out of the trunk.

Then Valerie balked. Some part of her mind recognized that going to Granny's house stoned, in the company of the ominously capable stranger who got her that way, was not going to get her a warm welcome. And Valerie was a girl who, having been granted a great many favors as she grew, now expected the path to be made smooth for her. Valerie didn't suffer rejection, she dispensed it.

'I changed my mind,' she said. 'Turn around.'

Robin half expected that a smile might break his face right then, but he summoned one from somewhere as he bent toward Valerie, said, 'OK,' and kissed her lightly on the lips. *God, the smell.*

'Just give me a minute alone with silly old Zeb,' he said, turning off the motor right there in the street, putting on the brake. 'Then we'll go get a great big pizza with everything,' he smiled wider, 'and take it to your place with a lot of beer and eat naked. What do you say?'

That put a whole new face on the plan, and on Valerie. 'What I say, Dicky Boy,' she said, purring like a happy cat, 'is that I'm starting to think you are kind of a find.'

TWENTY-ONE

The price he had to pay for all the good meals he was eating, Zeb understood now, was that a couple of times a week he had to take Doris grocery shopping, which was about as much fun as a cold-water enema. She was picky about quality and she wanted to be sure she got value, so instead of just tossing things into a cart she read all the labels, debated the relative merits of competing brands, and consulted often with meat cutters and the people stocking produce. He suspected her of enjoying the process and wanting it to last, which probably wasn't a crime but was so opposite to how he felt about it that it almost gave him a rash.

He was feeling cranky anyway because she'd been on his case about a couple of tools he forgot and left out of the shed. He'd been shifting boxes around, taking a lot of stuff off shelves to find a quilt she wanted to mend with that thread she just got at Walmart. All the way to Walmart to buy some thread, could you believe it? And in the store, standing at the thread rack with a piece of fabric comparing, choosing, didn't she care that she was already old and the earth had turned several times since she began to look at thread colors?

When she finally found the quilt she wanted in the shed he had to put everything back, but naturally it couldn't go back just the way it was before. She had to direct him, tell him where to put every box. It wasn't hard work, just annoying because she kept changing her mind. She really cared about keeping the shed neat, and when they were done she said, 'There now! Doesn't that look fine?' Zeb thought it looked just the way it did before they started. But Doris was so pleased, she fixed him a terrific salami sandwich for lunch with a wedge of cheese on the side.

After lunch though, as he was backing the car out to go to the store, she spied the rake and the crowbar. They weren't in the way of anything, just leaning against the front of the carport, where the shed abutted the house. He'd stood them up there, just for a minute, to get them out of the way of something he was moving and forgot to put them back.

As soon as Doris noticed them she had a hissy fit about 'tools lying around,' and 'letting the place look like Appalachia.'

Zeb said, 'Hey, don't worry, I'll get them put away before the queen comes for tea.' But instead of taking that for the little joke that was intended she got all huffy and said just because she didn't live in a palace was no reason her things couldn't be treated with respect. So by the time they got to the grocery store nobody in the car was talking about anything but the essentials.

Zeb pushed the cart and reached down the high things. There were long waits in the aisle while she made decisions, more as she carefully crossed items off a list held two inches from her eyes. Zeb got an inner vision of himself as one of a long line of leaf-cutter ants, carrying his precious fragment along a tree limb toward a distant nest.

By the time he got the groceries loaded in the Buick, his mouth felt like the desert and he couldn't remember a single food item he liked at all. Doris was cheerful now, though – shopping perked her up and she remarked on the freshness of lettuce and the price of bread. When they were nearly home, she said, 'Let's put these things away fast and read a couple of chapters of our story before I have to start cooking.'

'OK by me.' In fact, it was more than OK, it was very good news. To his surprise, Zeb had been pulled right into the story of the failing English merchant in Cuba and was crazy about the daughter in the book, Milly. He saw that she was willful and gave her father a lot of worry, but she was beautiful and loving and he wanted her to enjoy her pony in peace. He feared the advances of the devious Captain Segura, and was afraid her father wasn't clever enough to fool the spies.

Doris said *Our Man in Havana* was an amusing satire. Zeb didn't know what that meant but he liked the story. Anxious to find out what happened next he went right to work when they got home. And as fast as he carried sacks in, Doris put stuff away. At home, she wasn't making decisions any more and she knew where stuff went, so she sped up.

When he came out of the house for the last two bags, he blinked when he saw Valerie's car parked a couple of car lengths away. Or rather not parked, just stopped in the right lane. There was very little traffic in the streets around Doris' house so the car hadn't caused any problems so far, but why was Valerie just sitting out there?

And how in holy hell could that be Robin coming from her car?

Zeb stood still by the open trunk of the Buick and watched with his mouth open as Robin walked up to him, smiling. It was a funny smile, though, kind of frozen there, not at all heart-warming.

'So this is where you ran to,' Robin said. The smile was still pasted on his face but it was making Zeb shiver now. For one thing it didn't match the eyes, which had that glittery sheen they'd had when he first got out of prison. So when Robin reached out to him, instead of taking his hand Zeb backed away.

The smile turned mocking then and Robin said, 'I need your car, gimme the keys.' He said it casually, in that way he had of saying or doing the most shocking thing in a matter-of-fact way, so you were thrown off balance and just did as he said. It was one of his oldest tricks; Zeb knew it well.

It had always worked on him before but Zeb was older since Monday. He had run from the stash house in terror, faced the fact that he was not cut out for a life of crime, and he wasn't about to quit being sorry as he read the accounts of the four men who died in the invasion. So he shook his head and said, 'Not my car.'

It didn't work, of course – Robin didn't give a holy shit whose car it was. He didn't even bother to argue, just said, 'Give me the fucking *keys*, Zeb.' He was getting angry about the delay so now he would inflict more pain than necessary to get what he wanted, because now he would enjoy doing it. Zeb knew that and got braced to stand the pain, since he knew he had scant hope of fending off any of Robin's attacks.

But then two more things happened at once. A Crown Victoria edged around Valerie's car and came to a stop at the bottom of the carport, and Doris came out of the house with her hand in her apron pocket, saying, 'What's going on?'

A man and a woman got out of the Crown Vic, said something to each other across the car and walked toward them. Wait, they were pulling guns out from under their jackets – what was that all about? Doris paid no attention to them, just walked up to Robin, squinting, and asked him, in a voice Zeb had never heard her use before, 'Who are you?'

Robin turned his cruel smile toward her and said, 'I bet you're Valerie's Gram.' He had his back to the Crown Vic, hadn't seen it yet, but only had to take one step to get his left arm around Doris, pull her up tight against him and clamp her there securely while he threatened her with his right hand, which suddenly held the very small pistol he had shown Zeb before the home invasion. Doris gave a little squeak of alarm and began to squirm, trying to get loose.

But both of the people from the Crown Vic had guns in their hands, too, and were braced a few feet away now pointing them at Robin and Zeb, shouting, 'Police! Put the gun down!' When Robin turned, surprised for once but still holding Doris with the gun in her ear, the woman yelled, 'Put the gun down now!'

But Robin would never do that, Zeb thought – he was going to use Doris as a shield to help him escape and it didn't matter at all to him if she was alive or dead while he did that. He was already starting one of his bold maneuvers, walking toward the two people with badges instead of away, saying, 'You people back up and put your guns down or I'll kill her right now.'

But as he made that move he passed in front of Zeb and in that two seconds, the last two he would ever get to do something right, Zeb grabbed the crowbar from the side of the shed and brought it crashing down on Robin's elbow, the one holding the gun, the only part he could reach without maybe hitting Doris. He knew his moving would force the plain-clothes detectives to shoot him – how could they not? But he saw the Derringer fly from Robin's hand and dove for it.

Then all the guns in the world seemed to speak at once. Zeb had one blinding, transcendent moment in which he thought he saw how he could do it all better the next time, and then something hit him in the head and he was gone.

TWENTY-TWO

Testimonials and conferences with the lawyers took up the whole morning Friday. At one o'clock the chief sent up a couple of pizzas, 'to celebrate your crew's fund-raising skills,' his note said. 'Congratulations to you all on a job well done.' There was a postscript: 'Ask for any help you need as you wrap up this difficult case.'

'Oh, yeah,' Jason said. 'Thanks a million for all that fine work – now go sit in the corner while we decide if you're fit to be a cop.' It was his first administrative leave and he was feeling the implied slight.

'Hey, don't take it personally,' Delaney said.

'What other way is there to take it?'

'It's just a protocol they have to work through. Be grateful – it keeps the cop-haters from crying foul. You'll get cleared by a review board of your peers and that will be the end of it.'

'Think of it as a paid vacation,' Ollie said.

'Which I'm really ready for,' Sarah said. 'Is it my imagination or was Thursday three days long?'

'You're not wrong,' Ollie said. 'And Monday was longer than that. We have passed through a period of flex-days.'

'And the best remedy for that,' Ray said, 'is luckily right here in front of us. Why are we letting good pizza cool in boxes? Come on, Sarah. Comfort food.' He knew they both felt the way everybody did, going on administrative leave – in a word, angry. No use going on and on about it, though – it was a righteous shoot; they had good clean records and a loyal crew to attest to how long and hard they had chased the murderer they finally killed.

But, oh damn, it would be good when it was over.

They all ate hearty – they had the appetites you get from putting in monster weeks, and they knew there was no point in waiting for the advent of perfect justice before enjoying what there was to enjoy. Dumping her greasy garbage when the feast was over, Sarah asked Jason, 'You ready to go to the hospital?'

'If you are. I'd just as soon get this interrogation done before I go on leave, wouldn't you?'

'Yes. If we wait till we come back we have to go over all our notes again to remember everything.' It was true, but she still longed to skip it and go home. Robin had been a clear case of a personality gone rogue. All along she'd expected they would have to kill him to stop him. Zeb seemed like one ambivalence too many at the end of a long week.

In the parking lot Jason looked over her shoulder while he asked, 'How about . . . Would you ride down to St Mary's with me? We have to come back to the station anyway to check out.'

Sarah watched him for a minute, said, 'Sure,' and got in his car. *Does he understand I'm not wise enough to be a mentor? Damn.*

Driving away from the station, she asked him, 'This your first kill?' No use pussyfooting around it. *He wants to talk – let's talk.*

'Yes. You?'

'Third. In sixteen years, though.'

'Well, does it get any easier?'

'No. Well, one thing's easier, I know now I can survive how it makes me feel. But it still makes me feel like shit.'

'Really? You too?'

'I'd be ashamed if it didn't. Who am I to play God? Except it's my job.'

'Yeah. There's that.' He drove well and it seemed to settle him down. Doing one thing expertly gave him more courage to stumble through the other thing. *Or maybe it's just that we're both looking through the windshield so we don't have to make eye contact.* He was silent a minute, thinking how to say it. 'I'm kind of . . . surprised at myself,' he said. 'You know, it's not easy being black in this society. I know that sounds like a cliché, but . . . my mother never found a man who would stay. My brothers and I had three different fathers. Two of my cousins are in prison right now. I'm not saying I was raised in the street – my mother did her level best,

still does. But . . . I thought I'd had a rough enough ride so
I was fully prepared to take the tough stuff in stride, you
know?'

'Jason, the guy we killed yesterday was fully prepared for
the tough stuff. That's the kind of person full preparation
makes you into: ready to use an old woman as a body shield.
I don't think you want that.'

'God, no.'

'So this is the choice police work offers you – keep your
humanity and suffer when you have to do hard things, or grow
a crust and take the tough stuff in stride.'

He tried a joke. 'So you'll understand if I suck my thumb
and cry?'

'As long as you don't wipe anything off on me.' They
chuckled, but the world didn't change. They rode a block in
silence before she said, 'It's not really a choice for me, and I
don't think it is for you. We need the joy that's in life if you
reach for it, people to love. Those things make you vulnerable
but they make life worth living.'

Jason turned in at St Mary's and found a parking place.
He sat with the keys in his hand, staring out the window, all
his usual bops and tics quieted now by the depth of his
thinking. 'I love being a sworn police officer. That's what I
like to call it in my mind, you know? It has so much . . .
substance. I took an oath. Something solid to rely on, that
nobody can take away from me – that's what I thought when
I joined the force. Well, I still think that. But yesterday and
today, for the first time I realized what a high price I am
going to pay for that.'

'We still have a critical incident debriefing to do, and you
can get all the counseling you need after that.'

'Those things help you?'

'Not very much.'

'I gotta tell you, Sarah,' Jason said, and with relief she saw
his savvy, cynical street persona coming back, 'you are not
exactly a ray of sunshine.'

'Don't ask if you don't want to know,' she said. They walked
up to the floor together, still carrying their Glocks and badges.
They would turn everything in when they went back to the

station, and walk through the world feeling naked without it till they were officially cleared.

On the stairs, Jason asked, 'This kid still has to face the music, huh?'

'Some. Depends on . . . oh, a lot of stuff that lawyers can argue about.'

'Like what?'

'Well, he admits to having been in on the prep for that home invasion, and four men died there, so . . . at the far end of the scale, there's a death penalty for even trespassing if it results in a homicide. In his favor, we know he ran away when the time came to enter the house. All the men who died were attempting murder themselves at the time they died. And Doris is suitably grateful for his efforts on her behalf.'

'Which really may have saved her life.'

'Maybe. More likely we saved her life when we shot the guy who was holding a gun in her ear. But we can testify that he tried.'

'Too bad he got shot doing his one good deed. At least we didn't shoot him.'

'I was ready to,' Sarah said. 'I fully intended to, if he hadn't lain down on his face when I told him to. But by the time we put Robin down, Zeb was down too and Doris was standing there with the Lorcin in her hand, crying and saying, "I'm sorry, Zeb, I'm so sorry."'

'And I guess that's established, isn't it?' Jason said. 'She shot Zeb? Not us?'

'The Lorcin had one bullet missing and Doris had the gun. She meant to shoot Robin, of course, but when Zeb broke Robin's arm and we shot him in the head, he sort of crumpled suddenly and the shot she fired put a new part in Zeb's beautiful haircut, right along the back of his skull. He's a lucky boy.'

'I understand why she went poking around her new roomer's bedroom and found the gun. What I don't get is why she didn't put him out after she found it.'

'She said he reminds her a lot of her own boy when he was that age.'

Jason rolled his eyes and said, 'Incredible.'

Sarah said, 'Here's an axiom of police work you can carry with you and trust: mothers are crazy.'

'That so? I sometimes think mine is, but I didn't know it was a universal rule.'

'Believe it. And now that I'm raising a niece I'm beginning to understand.'

'The stress, huh?'

'The conflict. Trying to discipline and cuddle at the same time.'

'Must be. Ask Mama why she goes postal over small things, she looks at the sky and says, "Sons."' He grinned at Sarah suddenly. 'All those bystanders we had at Granny's house by the end thought you must be some kinda Nazi, you know that? I could hear them whispering, "Why is she putting chains on a dead man?"'

'Dead man with a broken arm, I heard one of them say. I'll believe Robin's really dead when I see his autopsy report.'

Jason was getting better already, Sarah thought – making jokes about the scene at Doris' house. It had been a gritty circus for a while, all those neighbors getting in the way and nobody there to help them for half an hour.

At the door of Zeb's room they badged the guard on duty and signed his roster. Inside Zeb lay on the bed, his head wrapped in a pressure bandage. Considering he was in a hospital gown with an IV dripping in his arm, Sarah thought he looked pretty good.

They badged the prisoner and Sarah read him his rights. They told him their errand – to record the extent of his involvement in the invasion of the stash house. He expressed his willingness to be interviewed without an attorney present. He knew he had screwed up, he said, and that he was lucky not to be on a slab in the morgue alongside Robin.

Before they started, though, he wanted to show them a card that had been waiting on his bedside table when he woke up from a nap this afternoon. It said 'Get Well,' in big letters, and had some silly verse about nurses. What he wanted them to see was the handwritten message. 'Come back when you get out,' it said, 'and read me the rest of the story.'

*   *   *

Home by five on the dot, hah! Sarah parked on her side of the carport, surprised because Will's car was gone from his slot. He'd called to check on her ETA, 'So I'll know when to start the charcoal.' And she could smell barbecue smoke coming from the patio, but Will didn't seem to be around.

The door was locked, too. She opened it and went in, calling hello, but nobody answered. Aggie might be resting in her little house across the patio, but where would Denny be?

Oh, well. School mornings were pretty busy; sometimes they forgot things that needed to be told. *I don't want Denny going off on her own, though. I need to know where she is.* She felt odd, coming into her room at the end of a work day with no gun and shield to put away. She took off her blouse and dropped it in the hamper, and was hanging up her slacks when Will walked in and said, 'Hey, there.'

He was carrying two glasses of wine. 'This one's for you,' he said, handing it to her, 'for a toast.' She wondered, *Doesn't he know what kind of a day I've had?*

'Thanks,' she said, 'what are we celebrating?'

'You're supposed to say, "Here's to new directions."'

'OK.' She said it, drank some wine, and asked him, 'What new directions?'

'Tell you in a bit.' He sipped and put his glass down. 'Why are you taking those shorts out of the drawer?'

'What's wrong with these shorts?'

'Nothing that I know of but I don't want you to put anything on. You blew the Thursday morning date we were supposed to have by going to work early—'

'Oh, God, Will, I'm sorry. This case—'

'I heard. You can tell me about that later, too. Right now I want you to get naked and go crazy in bed with me.' He unzipped his pants. Some bolts and nails fell out of the pockets as he dropped them, and stood smiling brightly in his shirt.

'Will . . . Sweetheart, what about Mom and Denny? And dinner?'

'Sam took Denny and your Mom to a movie. Aggie's been a little down so I called her boy friend and he agreed Jack Sparrow would be just the guy to cheer her up.'

'*Pirates of the Caribbean* is in reruns?'

'This is a new one. They're having burgers before the movie and fruit smoothies after. We may have to double down on the cholesterol pills for a few days, but Aggie says it's worth it.' He took off his shirt. 'Is that enough information for you or are you going to stand there in your shoes and socks while your best chance for cheap thrills gets limp and shrivels up?'

'Oh, God, beloved,' Sarah said, throwing off her bra, 'come here to me.'

Later, quite a bit later actually, when the sun was a red ball sinking behind the cottonwoods, they came out to the patio, took out the roasted potatoes and put steaks on the coals. Sarah set up a folding table and they ate outside, listening to the evening sounds of doves. Will asked a question about work and Sarah said, 'After we finish eating.'

She ate the last bite of steak, sighed, and said, 'Any more of this wine?'

'You bet.' He brought the bottle out and poured, sat down beside her and said, 'OK, tell me about it.'

No evasions, no euphemisms with this man. She was never going to hear, 'How did that make you feel?' in dulcet tones from Will. He knew exactly how it made her feel to kill a man – like a pile of dog shit. And, at the same time, proud of herself – she had done what her years of training prepared her to do with enough skill to kill the murderer and let the woman he was holding fall gasping to one side without a scratch.

Since Will knew how that ambiguity felt, she didn't have to describe any *emotions* to him. She just reviewed how the case went down, from the horrific scene where he had brought her the snacks Monday night to the money in the floor, the guns and cars and more money outside and finally yesterday's crazy chase that led her to the bad guy just in time.

And then she found that after all she needed to tell him how she felt. 'I always want to make the worst ones my babies,' she said. 'I know that sounds crazy but when I see those terrible men with their dead eyes I want to take them right back to the day they were born and hold and stroke them;

make their lives so sweet they will love being alive and never do a wrong thing.'

'You're right,' Will said. 'That sounds crazy. In fact, it's just about the craziest thought you ever had, which is really saying something. Plenty of bad guys had nice childhoods and you know it.'

'I know. But something went wrong and the only way I can tolerate being in the world with them is to feel like if I had a chance I could fix it.'

'Ah, Sarah,' Will said. 'I love you, you know that?'

'I love you, too. Let's do these dishes before I get any sleepier.'

'In a minute. There's one sip apiece left in that bottle and we need to finish the toast to new directions.'

'Oh, that's right. What new directions?'

'I retired this week.'

'What?'

'I mean . . . you know, put in three months' notice . . . I can keep the shifts I've got till the last week in August. Probably take September off and start with the County Attorney's office on the first of October.'

'With the County . . . as a what, detective?'

'Yes. But it's different, you know . . . getting cases ready for court. I'll work Monday through to Friday like you, only not responding to current cases so the hours are more predictable. We can have weekends together, imagine that. And we'll have my retirement income, Sarah; we can buy this house right away, not have to rent any longer.'

'Wow. This is what you've been so quiet about?'

'Was I quiet? I've been working on it for a while and once I decided I wanted it . . . I guess I got kind of preoccupied. Sorry about that.'

'Wow. It helps with everything, doesn't it? Having more money and a better schedule . . . It's an interesting new skill set for you to acquire, too, isn't it? The other side of the law.'

'The end game. Yes.' He turned toward the street, saying, 'Sounds like the moviegoers are back.'

Sarah heard Sam in the driveway, saying, 'Thanks for the movie date, girls.' Doors slammed and Aggie walked through the carport onto the patio brick, heading for her little house. Yawning, peering at her watch, she said, 'Good heavens, that goofy pirate kept me awake after nine o'clock!'

Denny was behind her, giggling. 'Sam and Grandma both think Jack Sparrow needs a haircut,' she said, wrinkling her nose. 'I mean, they *so* don't get it.'